THE SPELL

Finding the Lost Magic

Trilogy

Book One

Layna Belle

Touch this page for

Good Vibes

XXX

ESTB  2021

Lilyleaf11

PUBLISHING CO

"The Lotus flower is regarded in many different cultures, especially in eastern religions, as a symbol of purity, enlightenment, self-regeneration and rebirth. Its characteristics are a perfect analogy for the human condition: even when its roots are in the dirtiest waters, the Lotus produces the most beautiful flower."

— BINGHAMTON UNIVERSITY NEW YORK

Contents

Prologue   i

Chapter One   1

Chapter Two   13

Chapter Three   27

Chapter Four   43

Chapter Five   53

Chapter Six   65

Chapter Seven   79

Chapter Eight   89

Chapter Nine   99

Chapter Ten   107

Chapter Eleven   117

Chapter Twelve   129

About the Author   141

About Lilyleaf11 Publishing Co.   142

Prologue

You must have heard about them before, women who existed long before we were born. Women who were wise beyond their age, who knew the time and how to stop it—women who could create and destroy. Years ago, these beautiful and powerful women existed. They were the women of wisdom. But there were men of wisdom as well. Some were called magicians, and some were called wizards. These men and women gave balance to the worlds, fighting evil and darkness and protecting those who had no protection, but that changed over time.

People began to fear them. "How could ordinary humans be as powerful as the creators?" they murmured. Mortals were not allowed to wield such great powers. This caused a fear amongst people and soon, children were told to fear the wise men and women. These children grew and told the same to their own children. And so, it started, the stories that placed fear in our hearts. What they did not know was that everyone held the same energy from the Source of where it all began as long as they were in this Universe. They were all taught that having powers was bad, and so they separated themselves from the source.

The wise men and women began to use their powers only at night, making potions and spells, to hide away from the rest of the world. But if they were found out, they would be taken away from their families forever and ever. It took a long time, but humans are now beginning to realize the true power that lies within them. But to unlock these powers, they need the key with which to unlock the powers of the Universe. And one must always remember that the power moves through everyone in the Universe. You decide how you use it. If you use it for evil, it will return to you. If you use it for good, it will return to you.

"Are we done for today?" Sage asked her colleague as the actors in costumes left the set. She saw one of the actors, who had the costume of an ogre on, as he walked past her, fuming about the makeup being itchy. He fumed some more before disappearing into a room. Pete. That was his name. Sage found him a bit frustrating. His energy was too dark for her, and he was always complaining about something. He obviously had drama going on. Sage tried to be compassionate, but sometimes it was hard when she had her own stuff.

"We are. Everyone will be clearing out in a few minutes. You can leave after that. Why are you in a hurry, though?" her colleague asked. They worked as assistants on the movie set together. Although Sage rarely spoke with him, he still tried to talk to her once in a while.

"Lunaa, my cat, doesn't like it when I'm late. She'll be mad at me. And it will be the third time this week," Sage replied with a smile.

Her colleague chuckled. They were not friends per se, but he was nice and friendly to her, and she noted the positive energy that always surrounded him.

"I can relate. My dog, Odie, does the same thing. I think our pets would make good friends. I wonder when it'll be Bring Your Pet To Work Day," he said.

Sage smiled. "I think so too."

She looked around. The workers in charge of the set had finished up with the stage. Sage checked that everything was back in the storeroom before signing out. She was in a hurry. As much as she loved her job, the creativity, and the beauty of it, it was demanding and stressful as well. If she wanted to leave early, there was one person she needed to avoid. It was the executive assistant, Harley.

More than anything, Sage aspired to be like Harley, as dedicated as he was. But that didn't mean she wanted to work extra hours. She gathered her things and shoved them into her backpack. Certain she had everything, she started walking out of the building, swinging her keys with her clear quartz key holder. She was almost at the front door when someone called out to her.

"Sage! Sage!"

Sage knew who that voice belonged to. It belonged to the one and only Harley. She increased her speed, walking incredibly faster. She finally got out through the front door. Sage glanced at the sky; it would be dark soon. The sun was beginning to disappear slowly. She closed her eyes and took a deep breath and, as she did, she felt a hand on her shoulder. Sage gasped before turning around to see who it was.

She was looking right at Harley. He was smiling and his smile reached his honey-colored eyes. Sage shivered slightly. Harley's eyes always seemed to sparkle whenever she looked at them. She swallowed hard.

"Hi-i, Harley," she stammered, brushing a stubborn lock of hair out of her face. It was a little windy.

Harley smiled. "Hey, you're leaving quite early again today. It's Friday. You need some time for yourself?"

At least he isn't asking me to get back to work, she thought. *I would have died right on the spot. I've been here for hours already.*

"It's not that. I need to get home early for actual reasons," Sage replied.

"But why? The rest of the team always says you don't like hanging out with them after a long day. I know you must have your reasons, but it is nice to spend time with people you work with," Harley said.

For Sage, having a good time was staying home with her pet cat Lunaa and reading a good book, or cooking up potions, and making spells. Witchy little things like that, that actually mattered to her. Not going out with a bunch of people that didn't know her well.

"Alright look, if you let me go today, I'll hang out with you guys next Friday. But I do have to get home today," she said, raising her wrist to check her watch. She frowned.

"What is it?" Harley asked.

"If I don't leave right now, I will most definitely be ten minutes late. I have to go, Harley. See you on Monday," Sage said.

She tried not to look at his eyes as she turned around because if she did, she would get weak and give in to Harley's request.

"See you on Monday, Sage. Have a great weekend," Harley replied.

Sage waved at him before she started walking. She stopped a cab a minute later and got in. Confident that she would return early, she sat back in the cab and relaxed. The drive home wasn't so long though, and she soon found herself getting out of the car, paying the driver, and waiting for him to drive away, before jogging up the steps in front of her house, in a hurry to meet

Lunaa. The house used to belong to her grandmother. When she died, she willed it and the expanse of land around it to Sage. At first, Sage didn't want it, but she knew there was no other person that her grandmother would have wanted to have her house and everything she once held dear.

The moment she unlocked the door, Lunaa came rushing for her. Her aqua-colored eyes that Sage loved went wide in excitement as she welcomed her back home. Sage gave her caramel and dark-brown streaked fur a good rub.

Sage's house was like a little cottage. It was one of her favorite things. The best part about it was that she'd inherited it from her grandmother. The house was far from the city and even though sometimes Sage had to pay a lot to get to work, she didn't mind. She'd been saving up to buy a jeep.

Sage picked Lunaa up before heading to her room. She dropped her back on the bed and decided she needed a shower after her long day at work. So many things had gone wrong in one day—the last thing she wanted was for something else to go out of place. There was too much negative energy at work. She would take a bath and then do a little cleansing ritual for herself.

Before performing any sort of ritual, Sage would try her best to calm her spirit and mind. Her grandmother had taught her that. She pushed away whatever trouble she had faced during the day as she took on a more serene and elevated one. Sage took a few minutes to meditate so she could be in the right frame of mind to create her sacred space. She cleared a space in her sitting room, then she used a broom and dustpan to sweep out anything that would cause distraction. She removed unnecessary things and then, when she was certain she was done, after wiping the surface area clean, she decided it was time to take that much needed bath. But first, she spritzed a bit of lavender and burned incense before leaving.

Cleansing herself was next on her to-do list. Sage shrugged off her clothes and folded them into neat bundles in the laundry basket. She needed a purifying ritual bath. She grabbed her cleansing bath scrub that she always restocked and applied it to her skin with a damp washcloth. The scent of lavender calmed her mind and eased her. When she was done, she got under the shower and washed off the salt, letting go of the negative energy that surrounded her as well. She got out of the shower and wiped herself dry with a fresh towel.

Sage changed into a big shirt and silky pajama pants. She gathered everything she needed and went back to the space she made in her sitting room. The incense was still burning. She sprinkled a bit of sea salt in the space before bringing out her candles and lighting them up before sitting down monk style.

It was almost half an hour later when Sage finished with her ritual. She had written down her intentions as she always did, and she was now cleansing her crystals. A black tourmaline crystal sat in the middle of her sitting room. It absorbed dark energy, and it turned anxious vibrations into positive ones.

Sage's stomach grumbled. She groaned and Lunaa groaned beside her, too.

"You want dinner too?" she asked the cat.

Lunaa let out a tiny meow and then yawned. When Sage got up, she got up as well. Together, they walked into Sage's comfy kitchen. Not wanting anything big for dinner, Sage decided she would make pancakes. She got the pancake mix from her kitchen drawer and poured it into a bowl, and then added buttermilk to it. She added mashed bananas and vanilla extract, toasted nuts, and cinnamon. This was her grandmother's recipe, and she had learned it at a young age because she loved pancakes.

"Lunaa, I think I should make a new recipe from Grams old recipe. Wouldn't that be nice?" She asked her cat as she flipped the pancake on the frying pan.

The cat didn't seem to care; her mind was on the food. Lunaa was a cross between an Asian Leopard and a spotted Egyptian Mau. She was mischievous, but she was loving and loyal to Sage. Although she had a cheeky sense of humor. Lunaa loved stealing socks and shiny objects. Her bed was full of them and whatever she stole permanently belonged to her. Sage had gotten new socks every week since the day Lunaa was adopted.

"It's going to be a full moon on Sunday evening. I'm going to make a lot of moon water. We'll visit Gram's stream, the little one near her garden. What do you say?"

Lunaa stretched tiredly. Sometimes, Sage wondered if Lunaa could understand all her rambling. She fried the rest of the pancakes, even though it was probably too many. She had an orange juice box in her fridge. She brought it out as well and poured some into a glass.

"Alright, let's have dinner, Lu," Sage said, piling pancakes on a plate. She added a slice of butter, topping it with nuts and fruits. She fixed a small plate for Lunaa too. The Universe forbids such an elegant and sophisticated creature as herself to eat bland cat food while her human ate something as delicious as pancakes. Lunaa's glare would have been enough to make Sage understand. They didn't need that; they already had an understanding of one another.

Sage took their plates to their favorite couch in the sitting room, then she went back to the kitchen and grabbed the juice she had poured into a glass for herself. They ate together, Sage eating quietly, and Lunaa chomping as quietly as she could too. After dinner, Sage got some coconut ice cream for dessert. Not that she really needed it, as dinner was already sweet enough. Friday night vibes. They cuddled on the couch and watched an old movie on Sage's laptop. It was 11:11 PM on Sage's grandfather clock before she finally started falling asleep. A bit of a warm breeze tickled her cheeks and ruffled her curly brown locks as she tried to make herself comfortable. Sage smiled. Her chest filled with warmth. Ever since her grandmother died, that warm breeze tickled her cheeks before she slept.

"Good night, Grams," she whispered as she succumbed to sleep.

Chapter One

)) ● ((

"**D**o you want to go somewhere with me?" Grandma asked.

At the sound of her grandmother's voice, Sage sat up quickly, awake. She wiped her face sleepily. When she sat up, she saw her grandmother in her favorite old silk gown, the one with the hand-painted wildflowers at the bottom. Her grandmother was staring at her, a smile plastered on her face.

"Come on now. They are waiting for us, and it would be rude to be late. Mr. Buttercup hates tardiness," Sage's grandmother said as Sage got up. She was still trying to process everything happening around her.

Her grandmother held her hand. It was soft, warm, and welcoming. Sage subconsciously held on as they walked through a ring of bright light. They were suddenly standing in a meadow, with a gorgeous fountain sitting in a small clearing at the center. The scent of wildflowers filled Sage. She could smell the aroma of lavender and honey, and she wondered where it came from. Her grandmother had told her stories of this place and now she was finally visiting it.

Mr. Buttercup was a beautiful white rabbit in a suit and tie. He was taller than Sage and her grandmother, and he had stories of worlds he had visited. Stories that her grandmother brought back to her. Sage's grandmother led her to a gazebo filled with plants of all different kinds. There, Mr. Buttercup was sitting at a table and sipping tea.

"Well, finally. You're here. It's great to see you, Sage. Come join me for tea?" Mr. Buttercup said cheerfully.

Her grandmother led her to a chair at Mr. Buttercup's table. The humanlike rabbit had a British accent and carried himself like some scholarly fellow. As she grew older, Sage thought him to be full of himself and snobbish, but now she could see that he wasn't at all. He poured her a cup of tea. She took the cup and sipped. Lavender, a bit of chamomile, and honey.

"The tea is nice, thank you," Sage said.

"Do you know why you're here, Sage?" Mr. Buttercup asked.

Sage shrugged. "I don't know. But it is beautiful and peaceful here."

"Yes, but it is not your home. The time is almost upon us, Sage. Soon you will be ready. It is only a matter of time now."

"What is he talking about, Grandma?" Sage asked, turning to her grandmother.

"You remember when I told you that the world is no ordinary place, and neither is the Universe? Soon you will come to understand. As Mr. Buttercup said, the time is nearly here. Soon, you'll be able to visit on your own. I won't have to lead you here or show you the way. Soon, everything will fall into place, and you will be connected to the Universe itself. You will become enlightened. Very soon. But for now, you must open your eyes."

When her grandmother said those words, Sage was sipping the tea Mr. Buttercup had poured for her. But the moment her grandmother asked her to open her eyes, Sage's eyes opened immediately, and she sat up. She blinked rapidly, realizing she was in her sitting room once more. Lunaa was fast asleep next to her while the energy in the room was so strong that she barely understood what was happening. The grandfather clock read 11:11 AM. But the only thing that brought Sage out of her confusion was the loud banging at her door.

"Sage! Sage! Are you in there? You little…! If I should eventually get through this door, I'll end you for good this time!"

Juniper! Sage thought immediately, the taste of the tea the rabbit from her dream had offered her still at the tip of her tongue. Sage swallowed hard. Was she actually dreaming? Because now that she was awake, it didn't seem like it.

"Sage! Just you wait!"

Grandma was here! She was holding my hand. I can still taste Buttercup's tea. It feels so real, but it isn't! Sage thought. Her eyes filled up immediately. The smell of wildflowers, the lavender and honey tea, her grandmother holding her hand and leading her through the meadow. It couldn't have been just a dream. It was just too real. How could it be a dream? How was that possible?

"Sage! This is unlike you. I'm getting really worried right now. Are you in there? Are you okay?" Juniper asked from outside the house.

Sage stood up, a little lightheaded. She walked to her front door, turned the key, and unlocked the door. She opened it to a furious-looking Juniper.

"Took you long enough. I've been standing out here for at least fifteen minutes. If you had neighbors, they would have probably thought I was mad. What do you take me for?" Juniper asked.

Sage rolled her eyes. "You're just a drama queen. You woke Lunaa up with all the loud noise you were making. If you're coming inside, then please do. I'd love to shut my door now."

Juniper glared at her before walking past her into the house. She threw herself on a peacock chair while Sage shut the door.

Lunaa stretched. It was almost as if she could feel the tension between both women. She got off the couch and left the two of them.

"Even Lunaa doesn't like you in the morning. You're annoying," Juniper said to Sage.

"Says the person who kept banging on my door this morning. You were supposed to be here at exactly twelve in the afternoon," Sage retorted.

Juniper gasped. "You were sleeping the whole time?"

"It isn't obvious? I dreamt of my grandmother. I miss her a lot, Juni. She held my hand and led me through this portal to a beautiful meadow. It was the most beautiful I'd seen in a long time. The best part was that my grandmother was there."

"Oh, Sage. Come here, you need a big hug."

Juniper made space in the big peacock chair for Sage. When Sage sat down, Juniper pulled her into a tight hug. She held her in place until she was certain that Sage would be okay if she let go.

Sage's stomach grumbled, making her release Juniper from her grip. She wiped her eyes and turned to Juniper, putting on the sweetest smile she could.

"Did you bring food? You usually bring food. Did you?"

"Last time I checked, we usually cook at your place. You're the witch with the recipe books her grandmother left for her.

You should be practicing and trying to hone your skills. I'm hungry and that's why I came here this early. So, what are you going to make?"

Sage chuckled. "You're just so lazy. Come on, let's make waffles."

"And Lunaa?" Juniper asked.

"She's probably waiting for the food. If she doesn't get food any time soon, then I won't get any kisses either."

They walked to Sage's kitchen together. Juniper opened her freezer and went through its contents. She stopped when she saw the bucket of coconut ice cream Sage had barely touched.

"When are you going to eat this?" she asked.

"Eat what?" Sage replied absentmindedly. She was busy with the waffle mix.

"The bucket of ice cream you left in here. It's probably in tears, from not being touched often," Juniper replied as she dragged the bucket of ice cream back.

"Drop that back where you found it and come help me make the waffles. Get the waffle maker and heat it!"

Juniper glared at her before putting the ice cream back in the freezer. She got the waffle maker and cleaned it before heating it. She brushed a bit of melted butter on it.

Sage and Juniper had been friends since childhood. Juniper had this healing energy around her that Sage loved a lot. During her grandmother's funeral, Juniper had been there with her. Some nights, Sage would wake up in tears, but Juniper was always there, no matter what.

"So, did you ask him out yet?" Juniper asked Sage randomly.

Sage paused. She knew who Juniper was asking about, but she didn't know how to answer. Sage had told Juniper about her little crush on Harley. Now Juniper was all up in her business.

"No, Juni. I didn't know how to. I don't think I want to have anything serious with anyone right now," Sage replied.

"What!" Juniper replied, feigning shock. "You really haven't asked him out yet? What are you busy waiting for? For someone else to ask him?"

Sage stabbed a piece of waffle, dripping with maple syrup, and shoved it into her mouth, completely ignoring Juniper's questions. Even though she wanted Juniper around, she wanted to process everything that had taken place in her dream. Would she really even call it a dream? It felt too real. It wasn't astral projection either. Sage had not yet gotten that far. Her grandmother did it all the time when she was alive, but the only thing that Sage was willing to do was to learn how to make spells. It was what she loved.

"Look, Juni. I don't know. I've been hurt a lot, and it's time to start loving myself and just start living, I guess. Honestly, right now I could do with a walk in the park after we're done eating," Sage said, stabbing another piece of waffle with her fork and passing it to Lunaa who had run into the kitchen once she was certain the waffles were ready.

"You don't seem okay, you know. Is it cause you saw Grams? I know you miss her a lot," Juniper replied.

She dropped her fork and pulled a teary-eyed Sage into another hug. They resumed eating seconds later.

The best thing about living a few miles away from town was the peace and quiet that Sage always had. After their brunch, Sage had showered and changed into something perfect for the sunny weather outside, a sundress. Then she got her bicycle and, together with Juniper, rode into town.

The park was usually always filled with children and today was no different. Juniper spread a blanket for them to sit on. Sage laid on it instead, facing the shade from a tree.

"So, how's it going at work? You didn't tell me," Sage stated, turning to face Juniper.

Juniper sighed. "It's good. I love working at the bookstore. You know there's this group of kids that come in after school every day. They started a book club and they recruit at least one person every week. It's beautiful to see."

"You and I know you're not saying anything. You're hiding something from me. I'm not quite sure what yet," Sage said.

Juniper chuckled. "You aren't quite wrong, you know. There is something. More like someone, though."

"Huh? Really? Oh, my goodness! Juniper Holmes finally likes someone. I'm surprised. You turned down everyone who ever wanted to get with you and suddenly, you like someone?" Sage said excitedly.

Juniper laughed. She felt giddy. Sage wasn't wrong. They had attended the same high school. Juniper had been the fun-loving, happy, and full-of-life kind of teenager. Nothing could ruin her mood. Her motto was simply to be happy. Juniper could pull in a crowd. She had a great sense of humor, and she was generally a funny person. She was a bit whimsical, too.

"Their name is Ash. They frequent the bookstore a lot. And honestly? They are the best thing I've seen in a while, a breath of fresh air, if you ask me. But I don't think they'll say yes if I ask them out," Juniper stated.

There was a twinkle in her eyes as she talked about this Ash person. More than anything, Sage wanted to see the person that had managed to find their way into Juniper's warm heart.

It was a rare occurrence for Juniper to like anyone. Sage watched her move a lock of brown hair out of her face. Juniper was beautiful. She could have anyone she wanted to. She had blonde hair and tanned skin. Unlike Sage, Juniper was an outdoorsy person. She had a few freckles sprinkled across her face. And she had a radiant smile.

"Have you tried talking to them? How do you know you're attracted to them?" Sage asked.

Juniper shrugged. "Last time they were at the bookstore, they came to get a book about a green witch. I think they're one. Unlike them, I'm not a witch. Don't witches hang out together? I don't think they would want to hang out with me."

"What makes you think that? It's not true. You're exceptional and vibrant. You make the room bright whenever you walk inside. I think you can sweep a green witch off their feet," Sage stated. "And by the way, I'm a witch and I hang out with you."

Juniper chuckled. She picked up a piece of dried leaf and played with it.

"So, do you mean that I'm amazing? You think I can sweep a green witch off their feet?"

"I think so. I think you can do anything you want. Alright look let's make a deal. If you ask your green witch on a date before I grow the nerve to ask Harley on a date, I'll make you Grandma's favorite cinnamon angel cake. But if I ask Harley before you ask your green witch, you'll do anything I want."

"Why does your part of the deal have to be so simple?"

"You love food, especially if it's Grandma's recipe. I don't have a lot of things that I like, but if I can get you to do anything I want, it will take me a long time to make up my mind. You honestly have an advantage. Plus, I'm certain you'll ask Ash on a date long before I can complete five sentences while talking to Harley at work."

"Yeah, I forgot I was the cool one between us," Juniper replied. "I'll ask them out on a date."

"I just recalled something. I got myself into a tight situation yesterday with Harley."

"Hold on a second, really?"

"Yeah," Sage whispered. "I told him I would hang out with him and the rest of the team next week on Friday. But you know I'm not cut out for that kind of thing. I suck at making friends."

"No, you don't. I've known you for years and I've seen you around people you like. They're usually people with positive energies, people who vibrate at the same frequency you do. And when negative energy is around you, you like to shrink into a shell and not come out until something positive drags you out of that situation."

Sage thought about it for a minute. When her grandmother had passed, she had stayed indoors for days while her mother planned the "celebration of life." Juniper was the only one who could get to her. Her mother at least tried to sneak a black tourmaline crystal into her room every day.

"I know. You're right. So, I need your help escaping this one. It's a one-time thing, I promise. I won't do this again," Sage said.

"How did he even get you to say yes? You never say yes when I ask you to go out with me. I have to come drag your ass out myself."

"He put me on the spot, okay? If I didn't say yes, he wouldn't let me go. It was the only way to escape him, so I said yes. Will you come to save me? Be my knight in shining armor?"

Juniper laughed heartily. "Okay. I'll come. But you're going to bake cookies for me."

Sage chuckled. "Deal. You'll come to the studio on Friday. Be there an hour or two before it's time for me to leave. We'll tell Harley you have this family thing that I usually attend with you, and we've been planning for months. I hate that I have to lie to him, but I think it's necessary. I promise to bake as many cookies as you want after that."

"Deal," Juniper replied, lying down on the blanket.

Sage joined her and quietly said thank you to the Universe for putting Juniper in her life.

A few hours later, they rode back to Sage's house again. They had dinner together before Juniper left. She would have slept over, but Juniper could not leave her pet unsupervised. She had to get home.

Sage took a long cleansing bath as usual. She didn't make any spells, but she cleaned her crystals and her grandmother's mason jars in preparation for the full moon. She wanted to make as much moon water as she could.

When she was done, Lunaa followed her to her room. As always, Sage felt the warm breeze she had come to associate with her grandmother tickle her cheeks. She smiled as she whispered good night to it. Lunaa curled up right next to her.

At first, Sage could not sleep. She kept thinking about the dream she had the previous night. She thought about what her grandmother had told her and the humanlike rabbit that had been polite. Sage knew she had seen him before then. She couldn't recall when or where, but she knew she had seen him. In Grandma's nighttime stories, Mr. Buttercup sounded snobbish to her. But he didn't seem like it now. She sighed and closed her eyes.

When Sage opened her eyes again, she was at the table once more. The only difference was that, in place of Mr. Buttercup, was an older man that Sage did not recognize. Next to her, her grandmother was sipping lavender and honey tea. Sage blinked rapidly before closing her eyes. She folded her hand and dug a nail into her palm. She felt the pain, but when she opened her eyes, she was still sitting there at the table.

"Welcome again, Sage," her grandmother whispered, smiling at her.

"I'm here again?" Sage asked, a little confused. She looked at the man across from her and he smiled once more. It was just like Mr. Buttercup's smile.

"Yes, you are. Hello, Sage," the man said.

Sage blinked hard. Was it possible for two people who were unrelated to have such similarities? No, it wasn't. Sage looked a bit like her mother and yet they were very different. They had clashing personalities as well.

"This is Mr. Buttercup. He's a dear old friend of mine," her grandmother said.

If Sage had a drink in her mouth, she would have to spit it out. But she didn't, so instead, she stared at the man.

He grinned from ear to ear. "Welcome once more, Sage."

Chapter Two

)) ● ((

ondays were not Sage's favorite days. Maybe if Monday
had been named something else like funday, she would
have probably liked it. But Monday was named that
way for a reason. Every Monday, she woke up wishing she could
sleep in.

Sage sipped her cup of coffee as she walked into the studio.
She waved at the only nice colleague she had when he waved at
her first. Any other person that said hi to her got a hi back in
return, but that was that. The small talk people engaged in as a
way of socializing weren't Sage's cup of tea. She couldn't stand it.

Sage was in charge of the set on Mondays. Every Monday,
it was her job to check the movie set and make sure everything
was alright and nothing was out of place, but that was one of the
most stressful parts of her job because something always either
went missing or was out of place. Last time, someone had given
the wrong weapon to the main character. Another time, it was
the wrong costume. And it always happened whenever she was
put in charge.

The new movie they were shooting at the studio was about
a girl who had magical powers that she hadn't yet figured out.

They had only started shooting a week ago. Today, they were shooting a scene where the main character would go through a portal to a different dimension. A magical dimension.

Sage knew about other dimensions. She was certain they existed, so seeing this part of the movie excited her. But she had a lot to do and sitting around wasn't on the to-do list. The moment she dropped her bag and coffee, it was straight to work. Costumes had to be organized, and they had to be the correct costumes. She didn't want something like last time happening. She made that clear as she spoke with the lady in charge of costumes and make-up. Sage didn't like her energy; she seemed like the type that pretended to be nice. When Sage had had enough of her bad energy choking her, she left the lady and went in search of the team designing the set.

"Are we done yet? Is everything ready?" Sage asked one of the guys working on the set.

He shrugged at first, but then he turned to see who had asked and was surprised to see an annoyed Sage.

"Oh, ma'am. I'm sorry. No, it isn't. We still have to set up the rings…I mean the props that will be used as the portal. I'm really sorry, ma'am."

Sage sipped her coffee. Occasions like this where people acted in a disrespectful manner with her annoyed her a lot. But there was really nothing she could do about it. If she had known today was going to be awful, she would have filled her pockets with as many positive gems as she possibly could.

"It's fine, Jack. I won't report this nastiness, but can it please not repeat itself?" Sage asked him.

"Yeah. Yeah, sure. Look, I'm really sorry," he replied.

There were days when Sage would have tried her best not to talk to anybody, but today was not one of those days, and it irritated her a lot. The best part about Mondays was the fact that she could spend a lot of time with Harley.

A couple of minutes after the shooting started, Harley would walk right into the studio, and say hi to everybody like the easy-going guy that he generally was. It was unfortunate that Sage could never be like him. No matter how hard she tried to be nice, people's energy always completely overwhelmed her, and her grandmother would say if it was too dark for her, she had to leave because the fact that dark energy was known to corrupt good ones.

After an hour, Sage had to check the room again, just to make sure everything was in place. She met with the set manager, and they worked together to make sure the props were in the right places. Once the stage was completely set up, the directors, and the actors, and every other person took their positions. Sage looked around the room in search of one person. When she didn't see him, she assumed he was late, and just continued to watch the scenes with the rest of the guys.

At first, she wasn't really understanding what was going on with the movie until they got to the part where the girl with the magical powers went through the portal. Since it wasn't yet edited, she could only see the false excitement coming from the actress. Sage smiled because she wished it was real. She wished that she could easily slip through the different dimensions to different portals. Her grandma had said she could do it, but she wasn't so sure. Until now when she constantly had that dream, she was beginning to question if that was a lie or if it was the truth. Sage was beginning to think it was the truth because every night for the last couple of days since she had her last ritual, she kept seeing her grandmother in the wildflower meadow. And every time, it was with a different Mr. Buttercup. Except that all the Buttercups looked and behaved the same way, even their clothes, mannerisms, and their voice, were all the same. But they were not the same people.

Sage had so many questions to ask. She wanted to know how traveling through a portal was possible. Unless her grandmother was able to travel through portals or two different dimensions, there was no reason why she would believe it was possible. Now that she thought of it, it would be really exciting to be able to travel through portals. What kind of magic could do that? How could one transport themselves into a different place and a different existence? It baffled her, but she was curious all the same. Sage wanted to experience something like that maybe at least once in her lifetime.

"You okay?" someone asked Sage.

"Oh yeah, yeah, I am. I'm just a little worried something might go wrong as always," Sage replied.

The person who was talking to her was the nice guy with the positive energy. Sage blinked as she stared at him. She could see something like a white whirlpool around him; it was a bright color. Something wasn't right. It was weird. She had never seen that before. Sage closed her eyes and opened them again, just to be sure. She looked at him again. She could see his aura. She turned to look at the other people in the room. One of the actors had a really dark energy around them. Sage remembered how they'd stormed out of the set the other day. When she turned back to the director, she noticed that he had a bit of light and dark aura. She could suddenly see everybody's energy and aura. Some were bright, and some were dark. Then she looked at herself, but she couldn't see her own aura.

"Do you think the second scenes are starting anytime soon?" he asked her again. At first, Sage wasn't saying anything, and it made the man wonder if she was even paying attention.

"Sage? Are you here?" He called her once more, a bit confused as to why she wasn't saying something, and he tapped her. Sage snapped out of her thoughts and answered him immediately.

"Oh, yeah. I think we are. The director is ready for the next scenes. We are just waiting for the actors to be completely ready. The lead villain is still getting ready. I think something went wrong with his costume," Sage replied as she looked at him.

She wasn't really understanding what was happening to her. It felt like she could see two things at the same time. She could see the passage of time and the aura that was flowing around everybody. She could see the energy exchange when people were talking to themselves. She could see every little thing. The actor that had stormed off, whenever he talked to anybody with a positive energy, a little bit of his negativity would move towards them, and if the person wasn't really interested in what he was saying, his negativity would stay with him. Everyone who spoke to the actor could tell he was just filled with negative energy and so everyone tried their best to avoid him.

Sage got tired of standing, so she sat down. A few minutes later, the director decided to start shooting the next scenes. Sage was too tired to say or do anything anymore, so she just sat down on a chair far from the set and grabbed her cup of coffee. She gave it one look and refused to even look at it again. It was cold now and thanks to that, it looked like mud water. Frustrated with how her morning was going and not being able to understand what she was experiencing, she dipped her hands in her pocket and felt something hard.

Surprised, Sage grabbed the object. It wasn't smooth. She was certain she hadn't placed anything in her pocket, so how did that end up in there? Sage pulled the object out. It vibrated in her hands, as if it had an energy of its own.

17

"Black tourmaline?" She gasped. "How did it get there? I don't remember placing this in my pocket this morning," she whispered. It vibrated even more. If Sage didn't know anything, she would have dropped the gemstone, but she knew what tourmaline crystals could do.

While she stared at the gemstone, the pulsating feeling became stronger. She saw a dark cloud floating toward the stone. She turned to look around, in search of the one to whom the dark energy belonged to. When she couldn't find the person, she turned her attention back to the stone as it sucked in the negative energy. A second later, a bright light came out of the crystal. Sage nearly dropped the gemstone.

The only person who used to slip gemstones into her pockets, her bags, and purses, was her grandmother, and it started right from when she was little. There was something peaceful about finding gemstones in her pockets. It was a reminder of her grandmother. At the time, it was just something fun for her, but as she grew older, she came to value it.

Sage looked at the black tourmaline. It kept doing the same thing. She didn't place it back in her pocket. Instead she got up from her seat and placed the gemstone on a table not far from her while no one noticed. She could see and feel every vibration from the crystal.

Two hours into the shoot, Sage was getting tired of organizing items on set or making corrections. The scenes that she wanted to see had been shot already. She got bored and left the set. As she walked away, something came up in front of her, a box with four wheels. It rolled straight into her path and then knocked her off her feet. Sage fell down on the floor immediately, her head hit the box, and her hand got scraped on the sharp end of it.

"Oh my goodness, Sage! Are you alright?" a voice said.

Sage knew it was Harley. *When did he get here? I didn't see him come in,* she thought, but the pain in her hand and head was a little too much. She groaned in pain as Harley helped her get up.

"What were you thinking? Hey! You're bleeding!" Harley stated, his eyes wide. He led her down the hall to another empty room before leaving to go get a first aid kit. Sage watched him walk away. The graze on her head wasn't deep, but it was bleeding already. The scrape on her right hand was beginning to look bruised.

Harley returned a few minutes later with the first aid kit. He got on his knees in front of her as he opened the box. Sage was completely overwhelmed. She wanted to say something, do something, but instead she found herself avoiding his eyes because she would always get lost in them.

Harley cleaned the graze and disinfected it. Whenever Sage hissed in pain, he said sorry, but one thing Sage noticed was that he hissed as well, as if he was the one in pain.

"It's clean. But we'll need to use a plaster on it, is that alright?" Harley asked.

"Yeah, sure," Sage replied.

Harley got the Band-Aid and chuckled when he saw it.

"Is something wrong?" Sage asked him.

"Um, not really. I think the person in charge of making sure there's a full first aid kit at all times decided it would be fun to get a children's Band-Aid rather than everyday ones. I think it's adorable," Harley replied.

For the first time, Sage chuckled. Harley's laugh made her giddy with excitement.

"I don't mind having that on my forehead. It really wouldn't matter to me," Sage said.

19

Harley grinned as he peeled off the covering on the Band-Aid. He placed it carefully on her forehead, hissing once more when Sage hissed as if he was the one in pain.

The scrape on her hand was completely bruised now. Harley disinfected it before applying an ointment to it. His touch was so gentle, and he blew on the bruise to ease her pain. Sage could hardly breathe. She could barely feel the pain, not with Harley holding her so gently. It felt as if she was some precious jewel.

He finished and looked up at her, smiling when he caught her eyes.

"Okay, we're done now. Do you want to tell me what you were thinking while walking that caused you not to see the box?" he asked, slightly amused.

"I honestly don't know. I just know that I wanted to leave the room. I didn't see that box coming. I didn't think it was there," Sage replied. She took a glance at Harley and saw he looked worried.

"Now that I think about it, you could have been crushed. A lot of things could have gone wrong. You know that right?" Harley asked her.

Harley had this seriousness about him now. His eyes looked concerned as he stared at Sage. It was obvious. Harley was very empathic. Now that she thought about it, she recalled how helpful he always was. If anyone needed a hand or two, Harley would be there, waiting to offer all the help he could.

"I'm fine now. Nothing serious happened. Please, you've helped me out a lot. I'm grateful. A bunch of our colleagues don't really talk to me. I doubt any of them would have been willing to help," Sage stated.

"That's not true. They would have helped. It's not that they don't like you. They feel you're not into them. They think you are a loner and just like to do your own thing. You're not really interested in them or what they are up to. You could prove them wrong on Friday!"

"Aw, man. You remember."

"Yeah. And you promised. You said you'd come out with us on Friday," Harley stated.

"You think I want to hang out with someone like Pete? That guy is so negative, it took…" Sage stopped and restructured her sentence. "I mean, he's always saying nasty things to people. I don't want to be around someone like that when they're drunk."

Harley was confused at first, but he understood what she meant now. He shrugged. "Maybe it's you that's being a bit negative, Sage?"

Sage closed her eyes. She had wanted to say that it took a good amount of time for her gemstone to take all of Pete's negativity. Pete was the actor shouting and yelling at the staff members and it was beginning to infuriate everybody too. If she had said what she had seen, Harley would probably think of her as not tough enough and a complainer. Sage didn't want that.

Harley stood up. "I'll go put this back." He picked the first aid kit up. "Then I'll come back to grab you. Don't go anywhere now."

Sage chuckled and gave him a firm nod. "Sir, yes sir!"

Harley burst into heady laughter and Sage just watched, utterly mesmerized by him. He left the room. She thought about him after he left. She couldn't help smiling.

Harley returned a few minutes later for her. Sage's head throbbed, but she said nothing. They walked back to the set together.

"Oh, my. What happened to you?"

21

It was the nice guy again. This time Sage felt a little bad for not at least knowing the guy's name.

"Hey, Beau. How're you? Don't worry about Sage here. She got hit by the wheeled box," Harley said.

So Beau is his name, Sage thought. She was going to say something, but Beau beat her to it.

"Hey, Harley. I'm good." He turned to Sage. "I'm sorry. You're not the first person to get attacked by that box, I've been there too," Beau said, raising his sleeve to show a long faint scar.

"I'm sorry. You know, I honestly didn't see the box coming. One minute, it wasn't there, and the next thing I know, I'm on the floor. I'm just lucky Harley was around the corner," Sage said.

"It's no big deal. I honestly think you should go home. I know the cut isn't deep, but you might likely get a headache. I think you should rest," Harley said.

"I agree," Beau added. "It might not come now, but there's a high chance you might end up with a bad headache."

"But I've got work to do!" Sage protested.

"We'll handle it. You need to rest. Now come on. Harley, get her a cab," Beau said.

"I came on my bike!" Sage stated. She rarely used her bike to get to town because it was such a long way.

"You'll take it back tomorrow. Now come on, I'll book you an Uber," Harley said as he helped her up.

There was no saying anything or escaping from Beau and Harley. Sage had no other option than to go with him. He got her bag for her and walked her out of the studio where the Uber he already booked was waiting.

"Will you be fine?" he asked as he helped her get into the car.

She smiled at him. "I will. It's only a little scrape."

"Doesn't look little to me. Will you really come with us on Friday? I mean like, to the bar?" he asked again.

This time, Sage chuckled. "I'm not sure anymore."

"You made a promise."

"Sometimes, promises are meant to be broken."

After another long day at work, it was only right that she carried out a cleansing ritual, especially with what had happened at the studio.

Sage took a much-needed rest. She slept for three hours, with Lunaa cuddled into her side as always. She didn't dream about her grandmother either. When she woke up, she had hummus and veggie chips with a warm glass of cinnamon and star anise almond milk.

Sage started to prepare for the ritual a little early. She loved how she was at peace with her environment. The sitting room was her grandmother's favorite place to carry out cleansing rituals. She believed that it connected her with the rest of the house. Besides, the sitting room was one of the places guests usually stayed in whenever they came to visit. So whatever energy they brought with them stayed there even after they left.

She cleaned the floor of dirt and dust and then wiped it down with clean moon water. It would be a few days before a full complete moon, and she was nearly out of moon water.

With that done, it was time to have a cleansing bath. Sage cleansed herself thoroughly before jumping out. Her grandmother would spend long periods in the bathroom whenever she was having a cleansing bath. It was where Sage got her long bathroom habits from. Sage had to be careful about her injuries. As much as she wanted to be clean, she didn't want to get them wet. The thought of what Harley would say if he found out she wasn't taking care of herself made her tingle.

Half an hour later, Sage was ready. The moment she started, Lunaa came and curled up next to her on the floor. Sage loved moments like this. She started her ritual after she had calmed her mind. By the time she was done, the house smelled like lavender, and every bad energy she must have picked up was completely gone. Sage made fresh vegetables from her garden for dinner. Afterward, she called Juniper, and they spoke for ages.

Juniper talked about the green witch until Sage fell asleep to the sound of Juniper's voice. When Sage opened her eyes again, her grandmother was right there, waiting for her as usual, with her cup of tea in hand, and a different Mr. Buttercup sitting across from her. Sage was beginning to get used to it now, seeing different Mr. Buttercups and her grandmother every evening that she went to bed, for the last couple of days now. She was sure she wasn't dreaming anymore, certain now, that it was something else entirely, but she could never really tell because whenever she asked her grandmother, she gave her a different answer every time.

Mr. Buttercup had ears like that of an elf. He had long silver hair, and he looked quite young, but he had the same outfit as before—a green suit and a waistcoat with the painting of a tall temple that Sage didn't know about. As always he had a pocket watch hanging out from his suit pocket and he checked it as often as he could. His voice was still the same. She wondered if she had watched too much *Alice in Wonderland* when she was young. It was one of her favorites. This just seemed so real. But completely random.

He said hello to Sage as he always did. This time, her grandmother said nothing other than the usual hello to her.

"You're almost ready now, Sage. Almost. Very soon. You're almost there," Buttercup whispered.

When Sage opened her eyes once more, she was back in her room and the rays of the sun were coming in from the drawn curtains. Sage groaned as she got out of bed. Lunaa wasn't lying next to her anymore. The space where she would usually be curled up in was empty. Sage got up and stared out the window.

When will Grandma tell me what she wants? Or what this is all about? Why do I keep seeing her?

There was no one to answer her questions. Sage sighed. She had work to do, and she didn't want to be late. Absentmindedly, she rubbed her palms together. It was only then that Sage noticed something—her injuries were gone.

Chapter Three

）） ● （（

If there was anything Sage could do, rather than go to work today, she would have done it. But she hated being idle. It was a habit her mother had. She didn't really like working, and she lived a carefree life, but she hated being unable to do something, anything at all. Sage knew she had to work today. She took her daily life too seriously to ignore it. She did love working. Being on the set of movies long before they were released to the public always gave her a thrill.

Sage looked at the picture of her mother and grandmother on the bedside table. Her mother had named her after her favorite plant, the sage plant. It was a perennial, evergreen shrub that had woody stems, with grayish leaves, and flowers that almost looked bluish or purplish in color. The sage plant as far as Sage knew, was a member of the mint family Lamiaceae and native to the Mediterranean region. When she was little, her mother told her the plant was an antioxidant, and that it was traditionally burnt in spaces to help clear bacteria, and negative energy. Sage always hated her name, but she realized it was actually pretty cool and rare. She had never heard anyone else bearing the same name as her. Besides, Sage was different. Who wanted to be the same as everyone else? To Sage, that was just boring. She gave up on caring about what anyone else thought of her. It was just a waste of her precious healing energy. Her grandmother had taught her well while she was alive about the art of making potions with beautiful herbs and flowers. She had been drawn to nature since she was a little girl too. Sage got a few habits from her mother. She celebrated the new moon, full moon, and Spring equinox, just like her mother did.

Sage's mother had described her as hyperactive when she was little. But Sage didn't grow up to be hyperactive. In fact, she was a silent child. Her grandmother had been afraid something was wrong with her, but nothing was wrong with her. She was just different, grounded.

Sage stared at her palm. There was no bruise or any sort of evidence that proved she had been scraped by a big black box yesterday afternoon. The skin of her palm was as smooth as it had once been before the small accident. She didn't dare remove the Band-Aid on her forehead, afraid of what she would find there.

If the injury was fully healed, Sage knew she would have a hard time explaining to Harley how the injury had gotten healed all of a sudden. And to be quite honest, Sage didn't have the answer either, because she could not tell how her injuries had healed so fast. How was she about to explain the whole thing to someone else? There was no logical explanation for it. It was best to keep the Band-Aid there, just in case someone thought to ask her about anything regarding the injury.

She got ready really fast. Sage ordered an Uber but stopped halfway to get a box of raw sweet treats for Harley, herself, and Beau. Beau had been nice to her, she at least owed him some sort of appreciation. She got coffee for them too. She wasn't sure what kind of coffee they liked. It was kind of challenging with so many options and allergies these days, so she got them her favorite with vanilla almond milk. Sage was in a good mood because she wasn't in charge of the set for today. She could only watch from the sidelines and then at the end of the day, she would recheck if everything was back in place.

The Uber driver finally arrived at the studio. Sage thanked him for his kindness on the drive. She started to walk into the studio, trying to balance the coffee and sweets in both hands.

"Sage! I was certain it was you!"

Harley! Sage thought the minute she heard his voice. *Does he sound that way in the morning? Raspy and sweet.* Sage squeezed her eyes shut for a second. When she opened them once more, Harley was standing right in front of her, smiling. He had on a pair of dark jeans and a gray sweatshirt that hugged his fit frame. Sage knew that if he touched her, she would completely crumble into a mess.

"Hey, Harley. Good morning. I come bearing raw treats and coffee," Sage stated as Harley helped her with the box of sweets.

"Oh, wow. How did you know I was craving a raw treat?" Harley asked, opening the box. A welcome change to the coffee and snacks that were available on set.

From her side view, Sage saw something moving, it was almost glowing, a bright beautiful light. She thought it was weird and ignored it, thinking it was probably a bird that must have flown in through the door. Harley led her to the set. Sage realized she was already late, when she walked in, and the set was already set up for the day. She gave Harley a cup of coffee and then searched the place for Beau. When she found him, she called him over. As he walked towards them, something else caught her eyes again. This time, what she thought she saw had feathers or maybe wings. Sage wasn't sure, and she blinked again, a little confused. Why was it that every time she came to the set something otherworldly happened? What was it all about? What was the Universe trying to tell her now?

"Is that mine?" Beau asked, breaking Sage's thoughts.

"Yeah. You can have any you like. I'm not really big on coffee but it gets me going in the morning. I'm more of a tea woman," Sage stated. Why did I say that? she thought to herself. I love coffee.

Chad and Harley chuckled as they each took a slice from the box. Harley groaned when he took a bite and so did Beau.

"This is so good. Where did you get it? Is the store not too far from here? I'd like to get some for myself, more like, I'd like to get more of this, because I know I'll be sharing this with you both," Beau said, taking another bite of the raw treat.

Harley and Sage chuckled at his reaction. Sage took a bite of the sweet and groaned as well. She now understood what Beau was going on about. Who knew raw sugar could taste so good? Well, it's pretty much still sugar but life is all about balance. *Maybe I'll get some for me and Juniper, so she doesn't say I got all the goodies for my favorite colleagues at work,* Sage thought. She took another bite of the raspberry chocolate slice.

The scenes they were shooting were all magical scenes. There would be creatures from every different dimension since the main character would be traveling through them. Sage didn't have much to do, so that meant she could sit and watch. But Harley had to work, and so did Beau. Sage found a comfortable place away from everyone and sat down. From her hidden position, she could see the set, the actors, actresses, and every other person in the studio.

The scenes were to be shot differently but on the same set. The actors playing creatures had the basic costumes necessary, but something didn't seem right to Sage. Things had become incredibly different to her. She sometimes saw things that weren't there. She had thought it was just the light, but it didn't seem like it, because right in front of Sage, was a centaur—a living, and breathing centaur.

Sage looked shocked at first. Her mouth hung open as she stared at him. He did the same too, staring at her like she was something unique. This mythical creature that Sage had never seen in her life before had the body of a horse and the head and torso of a man. He stood around six feet and every time he breathed, a cloud of smoke came from his nostrils. But he had kind eyes and when he realized that Sage could actually see him, he smiled and galloped away.

Sage followed him with her eyes. She gasped when it hit her. Sage was no longer on set or even present in the studio. She was instead in the middle of a forest. It felt otherworldly. The sounds of birds chirping, the rays of the sun falling on the trees, the smell of the wild, and the feeling of dew drops.

The first thing Sage noticed was the winged creature that she had been seeing in the studio. She couldn't see it exactly, but she could see their wings now. It had a warm glow, and the feathers looked very soft. Sage wanted to touch them, but she was afraid of what might go wrong.

"Why won't you show me your face? Did you lead me here?" Sage asked it.

She heard a quiet, beautiful laugh. It reverberated through her and caused her to smile. She had never heard a laugh so peaceful, so calming.

"My name is Eli," came the voice again.

The voice didn't sound human at all, and Sage could hear it indirectly in her head. She could hear its voice. She found it hard to understand.

"You didn't say that out loud, did you? How come I heard it loud and clear? Is that possible?" Sage asked.

She heard its laughter again. This time, it felt like silk. Sage was very certain no one could replicate that sort of laugh.

"You can hear every word I say. I do not need to speak so loudly. Because I fear you might not hear me even then. There are repercussions for anyone who hears my voice through their ears and not their minds," the voice came again.

"Oh. So it's a bad thing to actually hear you with my ears. But now I'm curious. What are you? Why am I here? How did I get here in the first place? Where is this place?"

There was a light chuckle and Sage heard it. The creature flexed its wings and Sage heard the rustling of its feathers.

"You're never at the wrong place in life, young Sage. You're always at the right place. Do you know why?"

"Why?" Sage asked.

"Because you, my dear, are different from the rest of the Universe. Within you lies so much power, the power that could destroy the world, my child. But destruction is far from you. You, my child, were born with so much potential, and I have seen the things you can do. My job is to guide and guard you."

Sage gasped. "Does that mean you're actually my guardian angel? Is that what you are?"

Sage could actually hear it, the smile on Eli's face. She didn't need to see it to know that he was smiling, but he was.

"I am, Sage. I am your guardian angel. I was sent to you long before you were born. You were quite the stubborn child. You refused to be born."

Sage chuckled. Her mother had told her the same thing. She had spent a whole day waiting for Sage to be born, hours after her water broke. What was worse, her actual due date had been four days prior to the date Sage was actually born on.

"Do you have the ability to go back in time?" Sage asked.

Eli chuckled. "I will say nothing. I shall pay your question no heed."

"Okay. That's unfortunate. But I need to know where we are. I need to know that I'm not losing my mind and you're not a figment of my imagination. That everything that has been happening so far is real. It's a human thing. So, where are we?"

"Humans grow curious and more curious every day. No, you aren't losing your mind, Sage. You see, there's a veil over the eyes of every ordinary human in existence. But you are no ordinary human. You're gifted. You're more than just human. We're presently on the Isle of Indifference. It is called Division because, in truth, the creatures that live here are different, but they're united. Do you understand?"

Sage looked around; they were still in the same place. How could she get home from here?

"How did I get here then?" Sage asked.

"You ask a lot of questions, child. You and the Universe are connected. If it wants you to be somewhere, it will lead you there. It led you here."

"But I kept seeing you at the set! All of this is crazy. I won't lie, I'm beginning to think that I might have lost my marbles."

"You haven't, dear child. You have the power to do everything that you want to do. You're a powerful little human. You might not understand all of it now, but very soon you will."

When Sage blinked, she was sitting back in the hidden corner. She was in the studio once more. Sage frowned. Her meeting with her guardian angel had been something Sage didn't know could happen. Yet Grandmother's voice seemed to echo in her head. The fact that her grandmother had told her there were guardian angels who watched over humans from childhood, and it was true, made her giddy with excitement. What did that even mean? Was it a good thing? How was that even possible? Sage had so many questions and so few answers.

"Hey! You're here? I've been looking for you everywhere," Harley said as he walked into view.

"Hi, Harley," Sage said, his eyes holding her captive as always. "I usually come here when I'm tired of just sitting with the rest of the crew."

"That's cool. I have my own hideout too. I'll probably show you someday," Harley stated.

Sage wanted to say she knew the place already. That she had been there a couple of times too. She wanted to say it was the old speakeasy studio that had not been in use for a couple of years and the management was indecisive about it.

"I'm going to grab lunch. I think your new friend, Beau, might want to come too. Are you up for it? We don't have to use the cafeteria. We both know the food there is as awful as the chef."

Sage chuckled. The guy who cooked at the cafeteria on the second floor of the building was always grumpy. It really didn't matter who you were. The management had refused to fire him for some reason no one knew.

"Where are we going though?" Sage asked.

"Oh. John's pizza," Harley replied as Sage stood up. She grabbed her bag, and they both left in search of Beau.

Beau was extra busy. He suddenly had a lot of work to do. Knowing that if they had to wait for him, he would slow them down, he asked them to bring some back for him.

Harley's car smelled heavenly. It was so clean inside. Sage wondered if he took time to clean it every day. She nearly had enough money for her Jeep. Well, for the deposit then she would pay the rest off. She wondered if she would keep her Jeep as clean as this. Especially when she planned on taking it off-roading in the forest. She closed her eyes and sat back to relax, but as she did, something flew past her ear. Sage blinked hard, startled.

She sat up immediately, but Harley didn't notice. She looked back as something pillowy soft landed on her shoulder.

"Hello!" a cheery little voice said in her ear. "I bet you can't hear me!" the voice added excitedly.

"I can!" Sage whispered, turning to look at what was standing on her shoulder.

A little fairy in a small dress. She had transparent wings that glowed. The fairy gasped, surprised that a human could see her.

"How come? Humans can't see us!" she spoke.

"But I can. Would you be kind enough to not be naughty?" Sage asked.

The fae/fairy nodded her head, a little sad. "I'm sorry."

When Sage turned to look at the little fairy again, she was gone. Sage smiled. She had never seen a fairy before. Seeing a real-life fairy made her insides tingly.

"So, do you like pepperoni pizza? Or are you a pineapple on pizza person? Or the vegan type of pizza?" Sage asked Harley as they found a place to sit.

"It depends what day it is. Sometimes I'm vegan. Sometimes I'm all three, actually. I love pineapple on pizza, but I also love pepperoni pizza, and a bunch of other pizzas too," Harley replied.

When the person behind the counter asked for their order, Harley asked for a big box of cheese pizza. It made Sage wonder if he could finish it alone. But Harley said they would take the rest back to the studio for Beau.

Harley was a quiet eater, but Sage was able to hold a decent conversation with him. He loved jogging, he worked out three or four times every week, and he loved baking chocolate chip cookies.

"Am I getting a cake on my birthday?" Sage asked coyly.

"Sure. You will. Your birthday is the twenty-fourth of October, yeah?" Harley asked.

"Yeah, it is. How did you know?" Sage asked.

"I pay rapt attention to little details. You have no social media accounts, and you like it when it's really quiet. You work at the studio because you love creativity."

"Whoa."

"As I said, Sage, I pay attention to little things," Harley stated, taking a third slice of pizza.

Sage quietly took a bite of her second slice of pizza. She had butterflies in her stomach. Harley knew things about her. The urge to call Juniper and tell her got so strong that Sage dropped her pizza.

"Uh, I need to use the restroom. I'll be right back," Sage said.

"Alright."

Sage got up and left for the restroom. She got into a stall and pulled out her phone, but as she dialed Juniper's number, something changed. The room started to spin, but the only thing not spinning was Sage. She could see everything move with the speed of light. Sage's mouth hung open. Maybe she was dreaming. She closed her eyes and pinched herself.

"Ouch." She groaned, rubbing the spot on her arm that she had pinched aggressively.

"Open your eyes, Sage. You're not dreaming."

Sage recognized that voice. "Grams?!"

"Hello, baby," her grandmother said.

Sage felt a warm hand on her cheeks. The texture of the skin, the warmth that it brought, only her grandmother could make her feel that warm and safe.

Sage opened her eyes. It was her grandmother indeed. She opened her arms and wrapped the older woman in a tight hug.

"Oh, Sage. But I've been visiting for the last couple of days. Didn't you think that was me?" her grandmother asked her.

"I thought it was just a dream, Grams. I thought I was just seeing you because I missed you so much," Sage replied, still holding on to her grandmother.

"Come now, you were never dreaming. You were astral projecting, but you still can't do it on your own. That means I have to lead you."

Astral projection. Something Sage found scary, but she had been doing it all along, without even knowing what she was doing.

"How?" was the only thing that Sage could muster.

"Ah, Sagey, ever the curious little girl. Come on, we have to leave now. There are things you need to know about your past."

Sage's grandmother pulled away from Sage and grabbed her hand. Sage held on tight, afraid that if she let go, her grandmother would disappear completely, and everything would look like nothing happened. Her grandmother opened the door and led them outside. But instead of the restroom, they were in the middle of nowhere.

There was a wide expanse of land and not too far away from where they stood was a beach, its salty waters rippling as the glistening sun shone upon it.

"Where are we, Gram?" Sage asked.

"We are at the place where your story first began," she replied.

In the blink of an eye, they were standing on the beach, but this time, there were ships there, and a thriving city too. Sage realized they were in a different time. She blinked again and time seemed to move really fast. It stopped and now they were standing in the middle of a ship, where a man with curly brown hair and dark brown eyes kissed a woman with blonde hair.

"They found love at a time when their love was forbidden. Something so pure and beautiful. Your father's great-great-grandfather was the son of a witch, so he was a wizard himself. He used his powers only to heal, and he taught all his children the same. It became a part of them, and it never left them. It hasn't left you either."

Sage looked at the man again. He closed his palm and when he opened it, there was a bird sitting on his palm. The woman squealed happily as the man set the bird free.

"Come now. Come see how your father was born, hmm?" her grandmother said.

In the blink of an eye, they were gone. This time, they were on an expanse of land with a manor standing in front of it. The house was incredibly huge. Sage heard a woman cry and turned back to see a young pregnant woman being led into the manor.

"Who is she?" Sage asked.

"Your great grandmother, Leanna. She was the daughter of a rich horse breeder. Your great grandfather met her at a horse race, and they were married pretty soon after."

"You're saying my great grandparents were very wealthy?"

"Very. Your ancestors knew how to take care of horses and with that, they became a strong household name. They were no longer shunned by society. Instead, they were accepted."

"So, how did my father meet my mother?"

38

"Here. In this same manor. Your mother had come with a few of her friends. They were to stay for a short period of time, but your father was blown away by your mother and soon, they had you."

They were in a different place now, a quiet room. A crib sat in the middle of a room and in the crib was a sleeping baby. A single chain lay flat on the child's bare chest. The pendant was a gemstone that Sage recognized. It belonged to her grandmother. A small wind made the dreamcatcher move as it hung from the crib. The baby smiled in her sleep and subconsciously, Sage smiled as well.

"That's me, right?" Sage asked.

"Yes, Sagey. That's you. You were a ball of energy, child. You were everything both your parents wanted. But your mother had to go, and your father could never leave home, a curse placed on him from childhood. He was a healer, but he could not heal himself."

Sage frowned. The door opened, and a woman walked in. It was her mother, and she was in tears. She grabbed the sleeping child and hurriedly threw her in baby clothes. She packed a few things and ran out the door. Sage and her grandmother followed behind. They ran after her. At the door, a tall man with caramel skin paced back and forth. Sage stopped running. It was her father. Her breath caught in her throat. She had never seen him before. Her mother told her that he was gone, never to return.

Her father tried to stop her mother. He begged, but she ignored him and rushed out of the house. A cab was already waiting for them outside. Her mother got into the cab and her father stopped just a few inches from it. He balled his fists and yelled for her to not leave. His voice was filled with pain, pain that

Sage could feel. It burned a hole in her chest and Sage wanted to do nothing more than hug him really tight.

"I know, Sage. I know what you feel. But you have to see all of this. You were never really friends with your mother. That's clear. But she did only what she thought was right."

Her father ran toward the cab that was already gone. Instead, he hit an invisible barrier. It threw him off the ground and he found himself on the ground. He managed to get up all by himself before someone ran out of the house to hold him. It was his mother.

When Sage blinked, they were gone. She wiped her eyes furiously as they stepped into a different timeline and a different existence.

"I always wanted to tell you. But more than anything, I wanted to show you. You're not an ordinary child, Sage. You're the first child of a shaman and a witch. You're powerful. Within you lies the power to fix everything."

"How are you so sure?" Sage asked.

"Because I know. You know, your mother never loved another man. She could never. She felt that if she did, she would be betraying him. But she never heard from your father again, so she assumed he had moved on. That was why she never spoke about him. Look, Sage, to be able to fulfill your destiny, you must let go of all your fear and embrace peace. The journey ahead of you is a long one. You will make friends and you will lose some. But if you keep being the person you are, it will all be fine in the end. You come from a line of powerful healers and witches. The blood that flows within you is very powerful. You are more than you think you are. You just have to embrace your powers. Do good and push evil away."

Her grandmother let go, but Sage didn't. She wrapped her arms around her tightly.

"Don't go yet, Grams. Please!"

"My job is done. I must go now. I've shown you what I always wanted to. I've told you the truth. Your journey begins now. It's time for me to leave, Sage. You'll have to do this on your own now. I'll be here to guide you. That is all I can do."

When Sage blinked again, she was back in the stall and Juniper had finally picked up the call.

"Hello? Sage? Are you there?" her voice said from the other end.

"I am," Sage replied, frowning, and biting her lower lip. "I'll talk to you when I get home today. Are you still up for tomorrow?"

"Of course, I am. You owe me a well-cooked meal, so why wouldn't I be up for tomorrow? It's fine if you can't talk now. I'm a little busy too."

"Okay. Talk to you later then," Sage said before ending the call. She got out of the stall and washed her hands and face at the sink. She looked in the mirror. The memory of her father running after the cab, begging her mother to stop still felt fresh. The minute she saw him, it was as if, for a short minute, the gaping hole in her chest had been filled up with her father's love. Sage wiped her face with a paper towel in the restroom before leaving.

Chapter Four

>) ● ((

S age left work early after they returned to the studio. She wanted to make moon water and also do a ritual. Any ritual at all. She just wanted to get what she had experienced off her mind.

It would be a full moon night, Sage was sure, and truly it was. The full moon was shimmering on the water outside. It was pretty late and dark outside. There was a stillness across the land, and a slight autumn chill in the air. Sage grabbed one of her favorite crystals, a citrine. Citrines were known to radiate an energy of abundance. Sage loved it because it enhanced creativity and imagination and it also helped with manifesting any dream. If Sage was actually astral projecting with her grandmother's help, then she needed her to explain why.

Sage placed a beautiful piece of rose quartz that once belonged to her grandmother next to the citrine. Rose quartz was known to be the universal stone of love. She shifted the rose quartz to the right of the citrine. She felt like she needed to create a love spell for herself. Then she grabbed an amethyst crystal, another one of her favorites. Amethyst was known for its healing powers, especially where it concerned physical ailments, energy healing, and chakra balancing. They were used for protection and purification as well. Sage often used it to purify her energy. She had done a thorough cleansing ritual before now, but a second cleansing wouldn't hurt anybody.

Sage got a clear quartz next. This clear quartz was special because it had an angel aura coating. Sage had done this ceremony before when she was younger. She had made moon water to create a spell for change and prosperity. She wanted to leave her old life behind and construct a whole new person. Back then she didn't appreciate her body and how incredible she truly was, but now she thought differently. She loved herself just how she was. She didn't need to change to suit anyone or society's standards.

Sage added two more crystals. A piece of black tourmaline to ward off negativity and then she decided to use a piece of amazonite from her grandmother's old necklace as well. She had found an old mason jar and filled it with water from the river after she returned home from work. To optimize its effects, she placed her favorite herbs, and moonstone crystals, and blessed the water.

As a child, she had always loved roaming around the wildflower fields. The colors and the smells would overpower her senses. She would lay down on a soft bed of bunny tail plants and stare up at the clouds. She would see shapes and the more she relaxed, she could see dragons, mermaids, and angels, creatures of many kinds. These memories reminded her of why she loved wildflowers. As she shook the mason jar with the herbs and wildflowers she blessed the jar and set her intentions.

She lit her candles and set up her crystals in a sphere shape from East to West and placed wildflowers, herbs, and feathers in between. She wrote down her intentions under the full moon.

Would her manifestations come to life? Sage knew she needed to release what no longer served her.

After she was done, Sage knew it was the perfect time to cleanse her crystals. She folded back the paper in which she had written her intentions and stored it with a crystal on the top of her desk. She called in the powers of the moon and the earth to bless and protect her. She sat there with her eyes closed and breathed in deeply. Time seemed to stand still. The deep breath she released was long, and she began to feel a power start to surge in the middle of her heart.

She had done this ritual many times before but this time there was a shift. Something felt different. There was a strength, a desire, a power that she had never felt before. She spent more time connecting to her heart. Suddenly a huge rush of wind flew past her, brushing her soft cheeks. She could feel it swirling around her like a spiral staircase. All of a sudden, the candles blew out. She turned quickly expecting to see someone standing behind her but there was no one. There was only utter complete silence. In the darkness, Sage sat quietly. Waiting, thinking, contemplating. *Should I get up or should I sit? Is Eli back again? He's my guardian angel, so he's always around me,* she thought to herself. She started to connect with the darkness. There was a knowing deep in her soul that she was safe.

Just before she had set up her candles, she had made her special tea full of herbs for clarity—mugwort, blue lotus, kola, yarrow, and gotu. The tea had been known to relax and turn on mystical powers. It helped with cleansing and manifestation magic. Often, she would use other herbs to create magical teas. Juniper, tulsi, dill, dandelion, shisandra, and fennel. This time she had mixed a few of the herbs up by accident. She felt her intentions were stronger than ever. She had been focusing all week on protection and prosperity spells. Something was definitely different about this eclipse of the full moon. She could feel something move through her. She had placed the crystals corresponding to her intent. She didn't know why she had placed them in a sphere shape. Usually, she placed them in a triangular shape.

When it was time to sleep, Sage slept quietly, peacefully, with Lunaa next to her. She didn't see her grandmother or Mr. Buttercup or the meadow with the wildflowers, but she felt her grandmother's presence. She felt the warm breeze brush her skin like it always did every night.

Sage had left the mason jar overnight outside under the moonlight. When she woke up the dew had set in, and the mason jar had a soft shimmering glow. She thought it was pretty cool but was running late for work, so she got ready hurriedly. She took a shower, brushed her hair, threw on some clothes, grabbed her keys, and headed out.

The next morning, after the full moon, Sage noticed that Lunaa, her cat, was acting a bit crazier than usual. She was racing around the house like she had an extra energy boost that Sage had no idea about. Sage went to the sitting room, where she had left the crystals still in the sphere shape. She had her moon water from the night before in her hand. But as she walked toward the space in the sitting room, she tripped, and the mason jar fell from her hand, crashing to the ground. Suddenly there was a huge glowing light before her.

Her grandmother was standing before her again. She looked at the mess Sage had made with the glass and water.

"That was my favorite of all the mason jars I owned and collected, Sage. And you let it break today," her grandmother said as a luminous, transparent glow completely enveloped her grandmother with a bright whitish-yellow aura around her.

"You must remember, Sage, that the human species was designed to be in harmony with each other. They all have the same power from within. No one person should be seen as more powerful than another. The fear of losing their powers to those who wield them over others has created a dark hole over the earth and if you let it take over, then it can consume you. If you use the powers you have been gifted with for evil rather than good, you will receive negativity. But if you use your powers for good, you will continue to draw in more abundance, love, and happiness.

"Don't be afraid because, Sage, it's all okay. You are right where you are meant to be. You are a divine being, dearest one. Do not try to resist the energy of the Universe. It's flowing directly to you."

When she blinked, her grandmother was gone. Once again, she was confused. Sage cleaned up the mess she had made from dropping the jar and then got ready for work.

She pulled on a sweatshirt. It had rained in the morning, something that surprised Sage because the forecast was dry. She had burnt a few sage leaves in the sitting room the previous night, so the smell of the burnt leaves still hung around in the house.

Sage picked up a picture of her mother and looked at it. She understood why she had to leave her father, but they could have stayed together. Maybe they would have found a way around the curse, rather than leaving him alone. *He must be so lonely in that big manor, all by himself, unable to leave if he so wishes.* Sage sighed heavily as she got her bag.

She picked up her phone. She gave Lunaa a small kiss on her head, even though she was still acting a bit weird, before leaving the house. She got some raw slices on her way. She was still bothered about Thursday. It felt so real; everything looked too real. Sage couldn't possibly say it was just a dream as she usually would say. And she couldn't tell anyone either. She had to pretend like something weird didn't happen to her. But it was real. There was a slight bruise from the place where Sage had pinched herself. She could still feel a sting whenever she absentmindedly brushed the skin that was bruised.

"You're here early today," Harley said, hands in his pockets as he walked toward Sage.

"Well, I didn't have any reason to be late, so I decided to come as early as possible to this place of torture," Sage replied, laughing.

"Place of torture, huh?" Harley replied.

"Yeah. Place of torture."

"Alright. How are your injuries? Fully healed?" Harley asked, suddenly curious.

"Uh, I haven't really checked yet. But I think they're gone now, because the scrapes on my palm are gone too. I only noticed this morning," Sage replied.

"That means you heal pretty fast. If that had happened to me, it would have taken me weeks to heal and weeks for the scar to completely disappear. That's cool."

Sage just wanted to stand in place and look at Harley all day. She wanted to know what he smelled like in the mornings. She wanted to know if his hair was as soft as it looked. She needed to know all of that.

"So, are the slices for us?" Harley asked, nodding at the box of raw goodies in her hand.

"Actually, they're for me."

"Really? I thought you were trying to bribe me into letting you off the hook. You're coming to drink with us, whether you like it or not. If you say no, I'll get Beau, so we can drag you there ourselves. Besides, you promised, remember?"

Sage chuckled. She knew he wouldn't do it, but the thought of it was funny. Beau was a great guy; he really wouldn't sign up for that.

"Maybe if I bribe you with a slice, you'll let me go? I know I promised. But as I said, promises are often meant to be broken," Sage asked, opening the box.

Harley took a treat covered in dark chocolate and lemon drizzle. He took a big bite of the slice and grinned.

"Maybe I won't let you go just because you bribed me with a treat. But thank you, nonetheless, for the raw slice."

Sage watched him walk away. There was something about Harley that kept her captivated. But then, she didn't think she was quite ready for a relationship. She had been hurt a lot in the past and even though she really liked Harley, she wasn't sure she was quite ready to give herself to anyone again. The last time she tried that, it broke her for a while. Sage didn't want to deal with something like that again, so she avoided it.

She walked into the studio. Friday was one of the days with lesser workloads. Fridays were usually still long, but she wasn't always busy on Fridays. But she had to be here when everything was put away in the storeroom. She had to be here when their own studio was closed. That happened around 7:30 PM every Friday. Sage pulled out her phone and sent Juniper a text.

"Still up for tonight? You can back out now, Juni."

She pocketed her phone once more. She wasn't going to work at all today. She found a quiet place and sat down there, then she opened the box of slices, pulled one out and took a large bite.

Things at the studio felt different. Everything seemed to thrum with life. It seemed to vibrate. Sage would feel something move out of place, but when she would take a look at it, it was gone completely. She didn't understand anything that was happening, so she wasn't going to bother anymore. She sat back and relaxed, watching everybody else do their work.

Sage's phone vibrated in her pocket, and she hurriedly pulled it out. It was a text from Juniper. Sage rolled her eyes.

"We'll see. Remember you promised to make me a treat? The deal is on as far as you keep your promise, Sagey. See you at 8 PM. Meanwhile, my dearest green witch was here today. They bought a book about house plants."

Sage chuckled. She sent another text to Juniper.

"You sound like a lovesick puppy, Juni. You have enough house plants already. You have succulents, a round cactus, you're also growing an avocado tree inside your apartment, and you have a Zee Zee plant as well."

"Hey! Don't bring my babies into this argument. Look, they make me want to get more, okay? That's not a bad thing, you know."

Sage chuckled. Juniper sent another text that made Sage laugh even more. Sage had never seen an adult be excited about treats as much as Juniper was. She sent another text and then dropped her phone back in her pocket.

With nothing left to do once more, Sage relaxed in the chair. She didn't see Harley or Beau because they were usually very busy on Fridays. The only thing that she could think about was her father running after the cab her mother had hired. Sage didn't know when a bit of tear ran down her cheek, but she felt it when it dropped right on her palm. The room vibrated again, and this time, it was stronger.

After lunch, Harley sent someone to get Sage. She was surprised. She never really worked directly with him. She didn't have to before. She got up, deciding to go find out why he needed her.

"You sent someone to get me?" Sage asked the minute she saw Harley.

"Hey, Sage. Yeah, I did. Before you get mad, let me explain why I called you," Harley said.

Sage shrugged and dipped her hands in her pockets.

"So, the director says he might have to shoot a scene tomorrow morning. It just came up, and he doesn't want to shoot in the studio downstairs and the only other studio available is the one on the second floor…"

"Which means we have to get it ready if we don't want to be doing that tomorrow morning!" Sage said, frowning.

"I know you really don't work on Fridays, but unless you don't want to be here tomorrow, you have to do this today. A couple of others will be here to help too. So, what do you say?"

Sage groaned. "Alright, fine."

Harley chuckled. "You're the best."

"Great. I'll get to work then. What are we doing first?"

Harley showed Sage what the movie director wanted, and they got to work. It wasn't something that would take too much time, so by the time Juniper got there, they would probably be done. Sage tried to concentrate on setting up rather than staring at how Harley's shirt hung unto his ripped body. She looked away, a little flushed and embarrassed.

Chapter Five

》》●《《

They worked for two hours with some of the crew members. They still had a bit of work to do, but Sage decided to rest. She checked her phone. It was 7:30 PM. She groaned. She wanted time to move faster and instead, it seemed to be slower. By the time Sage heard from Juniper, it was 7:50 PM. Sage's phone vibrated in her pocket, and she hurriedly pulled it out. It was Juniper.

"Hello, Juni. What kept you so long?" she asked, clearly annoyed.

"I'm sorry. I know I'm a bit late. The kids were late today, and I had to make sure they had all left, including Kaleb, before leaving," Juniper explained.

"Alright. I forgive you. I'm on the second floor, in studio eleven. I have to work with Harley. They missed a vital scene, albeit a small one, and they want to do the scene tomorrow. We're currently setting up the scene," Sage said.

"I'll be there in a minute or two. See you soon, Sagey."

"See you, Juni."

Sage placed the phone back in her pocket and got back to work.

"Who called?" Harley suddenly asked.

Sage jumped a bit, startled by Harley. "Don't do that again, Harley. And my best friend called. She's coming up in a few minutes."

"Oh. I didn't mean to startle you. I didn't think you had any friends since you always run away whenever we invited you to go drink with us."

Sage sighed. "It's not about making friends. Sometimes, it happens like that. I can't help it. I can't hang out with people who don't like me."

"That's because you never gave them the chance to even talk to you, Sage. You could try today."

Sage brushed her hair back. There was really no arguing with Harley about the whole thing. It was hard trying to explain something and even harder trying to get him to understand anything.

She turned to walk to another part of the studio, but Juniper called out to her.

"Sage! Over here!"

Both Harley and Sage turned to face the door. Juniper was standing there in blue jeans and a big sweatshirt. She held a jacket in her open arms. Sage ran toward her and engulfed her in a hug.

"You came for real. I thought you were joking," Sage said, smacking Juniper's shoulder.

"I'm sorry. If the kids hadn't shown up, I would have been here on time. Now how long do you have to be here before we leave? Mum will be really mad if we're late!" Juniper said in a dramatic manner. Sage smiled so only Juniper could see it.

"I'm not sure. I might be here until eight PM since I've got a bit of extra work to do. By the way, let me introduce you to Harley." Sage turned to Harley who was standing right behind her. "So this is Harley. Harley, this is Juniper. She's my oldest and best friend."

Harley stretched his hand for a handshake and Juniper took it.

"It's nice to finally meet you, Harley. Sage has only good things to say about you!"

Sage wanted the ground to open and swallow her, but it wouldn't. Instead, she stood there, embarrassed.

"How surprising. I'm sorry, she hasn't mentioned you before in our conversations, but I did know she had a best friend named Juniper. Are you both supposed to go somewhere?"

"Yeah, we are," Juniper stated. She turned to Sage. "You didn't tell him?"

"I tried to tell him, but he wouldn't listen. I tried to give an excuse, but he wasn't having it either," Sage replied with a shrug.

"Is it somewhere important?" Harley asked.

"Yeah, it is. We have this family ritual at home and my mum loves it when Sage always joins us to celebrate. My job was to make sure she got there on time, no matter what."

"But she promised to go out with me...I mean the crew. Right?" Harley asked Sage, a frown evident on his face.

"I know I promised. But I did say promises were sometimes meant to be broken. I can't hurt Juniper's mother like that."

Harley frowned again. "Alright. But we'll have to finish up here first before you can leave. Okay?"

"Okay, cool."

"Can I help?" Juniper asked.

"No," Sage and Harley replied simultaneously.

Juniper shrugged and ignored them. Her eyes scanned the room for a chair or something she could sit on while waiting. She found one at the end of the room.

Sage and Harley went back to working on the set. Harley didn't say much to her, and it made Sage a little annoyed. She had to lie to him, but it was better than being in a room half full of people who had negative energies. The last time she had gotten drunk was in college and she made sure it was the last time it ever happened. She no longer drank alcohol or ate anything that contained it. But Harley would never understand. As much as she liked him, they walked on two different paths.

By 8 PM, they were almost done. Sage just had to return items that they didn't need back to the storeroom.

"I just spoke with the director. He listed a few changes he wanted on the set," Harley stated.

Sage stopped. "What did you just say? You told me this wouldn't take so much time and now we're making changes?"

Harley sighed. "I'm sorry this is happening, Sage. And I just noticed everyone else has left. It really wasn't supposed to be this way. Believe me."

"It's not like we can do anything about this whole thing, can we? So, let's just get to work."

Sage was getting irritated. Fridays were usually good days for her. Plus, she didn't have to do any annoying extra work. But here she was, dismantling props that they had fixed in place already.

By the time they were finally done, it was 8:30 PM. Juniper didn't complain. She just watched them do their thing. She played games on her phone until she got bored, then she walked through the room, pretending to be a character from a movie she had watched the previous day.

"Juni? Think you could give me a hand over here?" Sage called from the other side of the room.

"What do you need help with?" Juniper replied as she walked toward her.

"We need to get the extra props back to the storeroom. We can leave after that," Sage answered.

Juniper reached her. She looked past her and realized they were the only ones in the room.

"Where's Harley?" Juniper asked.

"He must be in the storeroom. Come on now, let's take these to him."

Wordlessly, Juniper picked up a prop she felt wasn't too heavy for her. She was shocked when she realized it was a little heavier than it looked. Together, they walked through the door and the hall until they got to the storeroom. Sage opened the door, and they both got in. She didn't close the door because Studio eleven's storeroom had a broken door. The room sometimes locked itself.

"Oh, thank goodness. I thought I would have to carry everything down here on my own," Harley said the moment he saw them.

"I'm not so bad that I'd let you do all the work by yourself. Come on now, we still have a lot left to bring back here," Sage said.

She dropped the prop she was holding, and it hit the staff that Juniper had carried. The staff fell down and hit the door and before Sage could react, the door slammed itself shut.

"Oh, my goodness. That isn't a good thing. That really isn't a good thing!" Harley exclaimed.

While Juniper was confused, Sage closed her mouth with her hands. They would be spending the whole night in the storeroom. There was no getting out of there. Not without the help of someone outside.

Harley tried to force the door open, but it wouldn't budge. It made Juniper understand the situation they were in.

"We aren't getting out of here anytime soon, are we?" she asked Sage.

Sage sighed. "No, we aren't. I'm sorry I got you into all of this."

"It's fine. I'd do anything for you. You're my best buddy."

Harley walked back to them. "I couldn't open the door," he said quietly.

They sat on the floor, all three of them. Harley tried to call the security guards, but there was no service with which to call anyone. It was the same thing for Sage and Juniper too. They gave up thirty minutes later and just tried their best to ignore the situation.

Sage noticed how calm and quiet the room was. It was suspicious. She glanced in every corner until her eyes caught something completely weird. The prop clock in the storeroom read 11:10 PM. The second hand began to tick slowly and as it did, the energy in the room buzzed so much that Sage could feel it; she could touch it.

The closer the hand got to its destination, the stronger the buzzing energy between the three of them. Soon it filled the room.

"Is it me, or can the two of you feel this energy surge in the room?" Juniper asked.

"I can feel it too," Sage stated.

"I hope this storeroom isn't haunted. I'll kill you both before the ghost gets to us. Do you both hear me?" Juniper asked.

In a normal situation, Sage would have laughed it off, but this wasn't any ordinary situation. What was happening was extraordinary and Sage knew it. She could feel it within her. Just like the energy in the room, her heart beat rapidly.

In the dark storeroom, a single glowing white butterfly danced around them. The butterfly wasn't like any Sage, Harley, and Juniper had seen before, so it surprised them to see it in the storeroom. Sage stretched her hand out, and the butterfly stood on her palm. In that second, everything stopped. Before Sage could say something, a whirlwind surrounded them, taking everything in the storeroom. The butterfly was gone.

Harley yelled for Sage and Juniper to hold on to his hands as the whirlwind carried them. With the whirlwind came a bright light that blinded all three of them. The light filled every corner of the room, completely enveloping all three of them. The last thing Sage saw was the clock. It was now 11:11 PM.

Sage blinked really hard. She couldn't see anything, no matter how hard she tried. Something heavy was sitting on her thigh. She wasn't sure what it was. She moved her hand there and felt the object, confused. It was a leg. A full-grown man's leg. It was Harley's leg.

Sage groaned as she moved the leg off her body. She stretched a bit and sat up, looking around. They were in a wide expanse of land. No trees, no houses, nothing. Just neatly trimmed grass. Sage rubbed her eyes two times just to make sure she wasn't dreaming.

"Oh, man! Where are we?"

She turned to her left to find Juniper awake and sitting up. Sage wished she could say they were dreaming. But that was impossible now.

"If I knew, or if I at least had an answer, I would have told you, Juni," Sage answered.

"This is the bluest sky I have ever seen," Juni stated.

"Yes, yes. But we need to figure out where this is first and then try to find our way home. So, let's wake Harley. Who knows how long we've been sleeping here?" Sage asked.

Juniper nodded thoughtfully. They both tapped Harley until he started to move. They watched as he stretched his body before trying to sit up.

"Where are we?" was the first question Harley asked when he finally sat up.

Sage closed her eyes and took in a deep breath. She knew where they were. It was a different world entirely. It was a magical world. She could tell because it vibrated differently from how Earth vibrated.

"I hope you believe in the existence of other worlds, Harley. Because we're presently in the Isle of Dragons," Sage said.

"The what now? What do you mean by that? What Isle of Dragons, Sage? We're supposed to be in the storeroom, locked in, and thinking of a way out, not in the Isle of Dragons or whatever you call it," Harley said.

Juniper stood quietly behind Sage. She knew Sage well enough to know Sage wasn't lying, that She didn't lie about things like this.

"Whether you believe it or not, Harley, we're no longer on the Earth you're familiar with. We are on a different Earth, with different beings, different creatures, and different beliefs. Whether or not you believe me is not my problem. Nonetheless, we need to find a way out of here. If you want to stay back here, it's your call. I hope the dragons are friendly when they see you," Sage said.

Without a word, she grabbed Juniper's hands, and began to walk down the field. Certain that Harley would follow, she didn't bother looking back to check. She heard him grumble a few times behind them, but she didn't say a word to him, and neither did Juniper. She was just glad that she had worn something as comfortable as a sweatshirt and jeans.

Sage turned to Juniper. She was quietly processing everything just as she always did. She didn't show any emotion on her face, but Sage knew she was trying to control her fear.

"Do you remember my grandmother's bedtime stories? About magic and things like that, Juni?" Sage asked.

"I do. I think about them from time to time," came Juniper's reply.

"My grandmother would always talk of mythical lands. I always used to assume that they were just ordinary everyday bedtime stories that adults told their kids to get them to sleep. But you know what, Juni?"

"What?" Juniper asked.

"I was always so immersed in the tales of magical beings, the crystal castles, and creatures that would excite, and delight me. I thought I would make a wonderful princess, or knight or even a witch."

"Well, you definitely ended up becoming a witch after all."

"A what?" Harley asked.

"A witch," Sage replied. "I'm a witch."

Harley's mouth hung open, but he said nothing to Sage and Juniper.

"I was so young at the time, and I would always dream of these worlds coming to life before my eyes. But as I grew older, all my childlike innocence faded away and so did the stories my grandmother told me. They became faint memories from my childhood. My grandmother died years ago, but do you know that I still feel her presence, her energy around me? She had been trying to explain that something like this would happen all week, but I wasn't paying any attention. In her stories, you arrive at the Isle of Dragons first and then you walk down the fields. The dragons do not like to be disturbed, but they are friendly and approachable. But you mustn't act out of fear, or they will definitely see you as a threat."

"How did your grandmother know about all of these?" Harley asked, the previous shock of finding out Sage was a real witch finally gone.

"Because, Harley, it is possible that she could also travel through portals into different dimensions. It's the only way she could know and believe it all. She never told me much except the bedtime stories," Sage said.

"How long do we have to walk? My feet feel like they're exhausted from all the work we've done in such a short period of time," Harley complained.

Sage and Juniper chuckled. They said nothing to him except to continue walking. Sage knew they would find the inhabitants of the fields if they stayed until dark and she was not about to explain to a dragon why she was trespassing at such an hour. The dragons her grandmother had told her about were calm and welcoming, but when they perceived danger, they could destroy everything around them.

Sage pulled Juniper closer. "Are you okay? You haven't really said a thing since we got here. You only helped me scare Harley."

Juniper sighed heavily. She hadn't planned to be transported into a different dimension, but here she was, in the middle of nowhere, far from home, and her pets. She wondered if they were alright, if they could cope without her presence.

"You're worried about them, aren't you?" Sage asked her.

Juniper nodded. She couldn't even call if she wanted to. There was nothing she could do to fix this whole mess.

"I am worried about Lunaa too. She was acting a bit weird when I left the house this morning, like a child that had too much sugar. I wonder if she's had something to eat, if she's sleeping already. Will she be curled up in the same place where she likes sleeping next to me? Believe me I feel how you feel, and I understand as well."

Juniper shrugged. "There's really nothing we can do to fix the whole situation. We just have to find a way out of here, and you have to help us get back home. Oh and I think you should talk to Harley as well. He's probably afraid he will never get back home, and he seems pretty shaken up by the whole ordeal. Besides," Juniper brought her voice to a whisper, "I think he likes you just as much as you like him. He just doesn't know how to say it, the same way you don't know how to tell him."

They were almost at the end of the field now. Sage let go of Juniper's hand and slowed down a bit so she could fall in step with Harley.

"Hey, how are you holding up?" Sage asked him.

Harley looked at her. His eyes held her captive for a few seconds before she broke it by looking away. Harley had this effect on her. Every time they found the eyes of each other, it felt as if Sage's heart was out of control. Her heartbeat increased and she suddenly couldn't seem to form words.

"I'm not sure, Sage. A couple of hours ago I was at the studio, getting ready to finish up with work, and go hang out with the rest of the team. And now, I'm in the middle of nowhere. Do you think I should be alright? I don't even know what actually is going on. I don't know where this is. I won't be able to get home. I won't be able to do anything because I do not understand what has happened. So Sage, tell me, do you think I should be holding up fine? I just want to go home and lie on my bed while watching a movie, Sage. Can you take me back home?"

Harley stopped walking when Sage stopped as well. Juniper didn't seem to notice because she kept walking.

"I have a feeling you think I'm responsible for what has happened to all three of us, but I'm not. Whatever happened, has happened, and I do not have an answer for why it happened, Harley. Don't think you're the only one whose life has been thrown off balance just because of this. Do you think I don't have a life as well to go home to? Or do you think Juniper doesn't have pets of her own to get home to? We were all thrown into this situation for a reason. We can either choose to find out what it is and fix it or spend the rest of our lives in a different dimension. The choice is yours, so pick one Harley."

Sage furiously walked ahead of him. She was afraid as well, but her grandmother had told her there was no need for fear. It was why she had been able to sit through those meetings with all the different Mr. Buttercups. Because she had learned to push her fears away. She knew this wasn't easy for any of them, but she had no other option.

Chapter Six

)) ● ((

They ended up at the end of the field finally. Sage stood there quietly, taking a deep breath. There was a small town there, one that her grandmother had mentioned a few times when she told her bedtime stories.

"Do you remember what I said about the Isle of Dragons?" Sage's grandmother asked.

Sage clapped her small hands excitedly. "Yes, Gramma. The dragons are friendly and nice, but if you try to hurt them, they will scald you."

"And then?"

"And then far from the field, the townsmen live. They grow fruits and veggies and play games at night. They will try to trick you, but you must trick them first. Only then will they help you."

Her grandmother gave her cheeks a firm pat, obviously proud that Sage had been listening at least.

"And how do you trick them?"

"I don't know that part, Gramma. You didn't tell me last time. Mummy didn't let me stay too long either. She came to get me the next day. You promised you would stop her so I could stay with you. But you didn't!" Sage said, her little voice filled with hurt.

Her grandmother sighed. *"I wish I could, Sagey. But I can't keep you here with me. You must stay with your mummy. You spend every Friday, Saturday, and Sunday with me, Sagey. That's enough for now, you know."*

"It isn't. Gramma. Mummy doesn't tell me stories as you do. She doesn't play hide and seek either, but you do."

"Oh, Sage! She has her reasons. Your mummy is afraid that if you play hide and seek with her, you could disappear and never return, and she doesn't want that. Your mummy loves you, Sagey!"

"No. You're lying, Gramma. If Mummy really loved me, then she would tell me why I don't have a daddy like the other kids my age."

Sage was smart for a five-year-old. But there were things her small mind would never really grasp. Telling Sage the truth would hurt her. So instead, her grandmother promised to show her who her father actually was when she was old enough. But until then, it would be a small secret between her and her granddaughter.

"I promise you, Sage, someday I will show you, rather than tell you why your mother acts the way she does. She made a choice years ago and you're the result of a beautiful love story. Do not think for once that you're not special."

"I am special? Really, for truly and honestly?" Sage asked in her teeny voice.

"Oh, baby, yes. Yes, you are. Now tell me, do you want to know how to trick the townsfolk?"

"Yes, Gramma. Tell me."

"Good. The townsmen know nothing about the outside world. They know nothing about castles and princes and princesses. They know nothing about all these. But they're little tricksters. If you are able to tell them stories that will either amuse them or intrigue them, they will help you. It is that easy. But you must never ask them a direct question."

66

"A direct question? What is that, Gramma?" Sage asked.

"It's when a question is asked directly to you. For example, can you tell me what time it is? That is a direct question."

"Oh, I get it."

"Yes. And now you must get to bed, little one."

Sage's grandmother covered her body with the blanket on her bed. She kissed both her eyes and her forehead before leaving the room. She didn't turn the light off. Sage didn't like it when the lights were off.

Sage closed her eyes. She took in an even deeper breath. Her grandmother had been right all along. This place actually existed so why did she think it was all a lie? Sage sighed. Completely exhausted, and tired of walking, she sat on a rock with a smooth surface as she convinced herself to stay calm and tried to catch her breath all at once.

Juniper and Harley caught up with her minutes later.

"What was that all about? Why were you walking so fast? Is something wrong? Is something after us? Are the dragons awaking now?" Harley asked getting closer to Sage.

Instead of answering, Sage pointed out the small town.

"There's a small town there. We could go check it out and see if they have anyone who can answer our questions. I honestly do not have an answer to all the questions you keep throwing at me, Harley. And I wish I did," Sage said, looking at him. "Oh and one more thing, every person in that town is a trickster. When we arrive, if you are asked a question, you must not give a direct answer, and when you ask a question, you must ask it indirectly. It's the only way to avoid getting tricked by them. The minute we are past all of the tricking, we will be able to get the answers we seek."

Sage stood up. She wiped the moss off her butt before grabbing Juniper's hand and leading them towards the town. The men and the women in the town seemed nice. The children played little games on the outskirts of the town. There was livestock as well. Sage knew someone would come to lead them to the village chief. According to her grandmother, this was the guy who would ask them the questions indirectly. Sage knew it would be hard to find answers, but even if it meant talking to a village chief in a weird way, then she would do it. Maybe then Harley would understand that she was not at fault, and she hadn't caused whatever was going on to happen.

They walked through the streets of the town as people looked at them. They only stopped when one of the men started towards them. He was small and had a mustache. Harley immediately took a dislike for him because of how he was looking at Sage.

"Would it not be exceptionally kind of you if you could lead us three to the chief of the town?" Sage asked the man.

The man looked at Sage and then Juniper and Harley, a bit confused. But then he smiled.

"Of course, it would. And you see, I'm indeed exceptionally kind, so please come with me!" the man said, immediately happier than he had been.

Sage shrugged as they followed him, ignoring the whispers from the people. The man led them through the town until they got closer to the chief's house in the middle of the town. It wasn't anything like a castle, but it was quaint and welcoming.

"Wait here and I'll go let the chief know we have visitors," the man said again.

The little man disappeared into the townhouse. Sage noticed how big it was compared to the other houses. Harley didn't look like he cared. He just wanted a drink of water, maybe something to eat. But he was afraid of what he would get if he were unable to ask for it properly.

The man came back to let them in. Sage could tell they were peace-loving people who never used their magic. She could feel it, but she could tell they didn't use it at all.

The chief was almost as tall as Sage was. He had long shoulder-length blond hair and his green eyes were pleasantly warm for someone who was about to trick them.

"Welcome to Littleton. It must be your first time here. Isn't that true?" the chief asked.

"We're sure it must be our first time. Wouldn't you say you have never left the town?" Sage asked.

Every statement had to carry a question. That way, she could easily confuse him.

"You mustn't ask such things to the chief. But of course, I have never left town. What has brought strangers to Littleton?" the chief replied.

"The same thing that has brought them in the past. Can you please tell us how it is that we're here and from where we must leave?" Sage asked.

The chief smiled. "You're very smart, I can see. What is it that you're called?"

"A plant is known as Sage. And what is it that you're called?"

"Atkin," the chief answered immediately.

Sage gasped, realizing that she had tricked the chief into giving his name. The realization hit every one of the town's inhabitants as well.

The chief chuckled. "I'm surprised. You're good. Who taught you to do this?"

Sage shrugged, dipping her hands in her jeans. "My grandmother did, years ago. I was little then. She made sure to teach me about your little trick. I thought it was just a game she played with me."

"Is your grandmother a woman named Eleanor?" the chief asked.

Sage looked up at him, surprised. Indeed, her grandmother had been here before. There was no way she could have possibly heard or learned about this place without being here. Sage wanted to jump in excitement, but she pulled herself together.

"Yes, my grandmother is named Eleanor," Sage replied.

"Ah. That is good. She did mention that someday, her offspring would come here. Who are your friends?" Chief Atkin asked.

Sage pulled Juniper to her side. "This is my best friend. Her name is Juniper. The man with us is named Harley. He's a friend from work."

"Welcome, all three of you, to Littleton. Our dragons are asleep at present; they're the protectors of this little town. We have food and wine, and we promise to show you the way you will go. We know you're not of our world and it is our wish to help you find your way home."

"We're grateful to you, Chief Atkin. Thank you," Sage said.

"It's no problem. You'll be taken to a room to rest for the night. You may leave tomorrow morning," chief Atkin stated.

Early the next morning, chief Atkin sent a message to Sage, Juniper, and Harley.

Chief Atkin was a quiet man, that was obvious. He didn't seem like one to go in search of problems. He liked his peace and quiet a lot.

A messenger led them to the chief's garden. In front of him, was a massive dragon. Her head was on his lap, and he brushed her scales. She was fast asleep and with every breath she released, a wisp of smoke came out as well.

"I'm sorry if this scares you. This is Bri, my personal dragon. She loves it when I let her sleep on my lap," chief Atkin said when he saw them.

70

Sage grabbed Harley. She had imagined dragons, but she had never seen one as big as this before and yet here it was, sleeping in front of her. A scaly lizard-like creature but it showed a softness and tenderness. Its wings were seemingly iridescent. Glowing with beautiful translucent light. The wings almost butterfly like. Its long tail ended in a curled tip and was covered in smaller scales shimmering with a soft tremulous vibration.

"This is not your final destination, Sage and her friends. You must carry on to the next part of your destiny. There's a portal in a cave that will take you. There, you can find your way home."

True to his word, there was a cave just like he said. If it would lead them to the place where they could go home, then it was only right that they enter it. Hands locked tightly, Sage, Juniper, and Harley walked into the cave and as they did, they appeared in a meadow, covered with wildflowers.

"Follow the path where the meadow leads," Sage whispered, "to find your way home, their words, one heeds."

"And the part only you see, it is the path where the truth must be," Juniper concluded with a smile.

"I don't understand," Harley said.

Sage looked down to find their hands still connected. She blushed shyly as she let go and Harley looked embarrassed as well.

"Gramma's late-night stories were an actual map. I don't know how, but I feel like I've been here."

"So, what's the way forward then?" Harley asked.

"In this world, there are castles and kingdoms with princes and princesses. It's magical as well, but it feels like the magic in it is dying out. Like something seems to be sucking all of it away," Sage stated.

"What do you mean by dying out? How's that possible?" Juniper asked.

Sage looked at the flowers in the meadow, and they no longer had their beautiful glow. They looked like empty shells.

"You know how a candle becomes dim until it suddenly goes out? That's how it is with the magic in the land. It is suddenly dwindling. I think the reason we were sent here is to find out why. Think about it, Juni. You're smart and you have healing energy, Harley is wise and courageous, and I understand how things work here. We actually make the perfect team."

"Well then, if our job is to find out what's sucking the magic from these dimensions, shouldn't we get to work?" Harley asked.

Sage smiled at him. "Grams said to follow the path. We'll definitely find someone to give us a lift in their wagon."

Before they could even agree, Juniper had started walking down the path. Sage and Harley joined her, laughing. Their fingers brushed together as they brought their hands to their sides.

"This reminds me of the movie we are currently working on at the studio. I wish they knew it was all real," Harley said.

"I wish," was the only thing that left Sage's mouth.

Humans would never believe in the existence of magic. They believed it when they saw it on their televisions, but Sage knew they would never accept it. The world usually stood against things that they could never understand.

"They don't believe in all of this. Believe me, Harley. They would rather push you into the darkness than accept your truth. Probably, if you hadn't been transported here with us and I narrated the whole ordeal to you, you would think I was crazy," Sage said honestly.

Harley didn't say anything for a minute or two until they got to a small road where Juniper was already waiting for them.

"I'm sorry. I'm sorry about everything. I've been awful to you even though I know none of this is your fault. Forgive me?" Harley asked.

Sage stared at him for a moment, taking in his features. She stood on the tips of her toes and kissed his cheek.

"You're forgiven," Sage whispered.

"Hey, guys! There's a wagon coming this way," Juniper yelled.

They stood by the road for a minute, waiting patiently for the wagon to arrive. When it did, they stopped it and asked the driver to give them a lift. He was a delightful older guy, so he did. They arrived at the gates of the city in an hour's time. Sage, Juniper, and Harley thanked the owner of the wagon before heading into the city.

"This is incredible. It feels like we're back in King Arthur's time," Harley said, grinning from ear to ear as he looked around him.

"Believe me, it is," Juniper added.

Sage said nothing. She was hungry, and they needed to get to a tavern. They continued to walk around the town for some minutes until they found a small tavern. Sage entered first. It was pretty much empty. A couple of people were already at some tables. Sage picked a table a bit far from every other table at the back of the tavern.

A woman came up to their table. "Welcome to Star's Tavern. What would you like to have?"

"What do you have?" Sage asked instead.

"Oh," the woman said, sizing Sage up before listing what they had.

Sage, Juniper, and Harley placed their orders and the lady left. As she did, Sage paid more attention to everyone around them.

"...the one who must not be mentioned was here. Rumors say she took the princess of Glendal last night..." someone said in whispers.

"...do you wish to die? Naming her like that brings curses and ill-luck to one..."

Sage looked at Harley and then Juniper. They nodded as if to let her know they had heard everything as well.

"... she's slowly taking the life force from the Isle of Man. It won't be long until we become like the Isle of Joy..." another man added.

"I'm afraid, no one will be able to stop her ever. She grows powerful by the hour."

The lady brought the food for Sage, Juniper, and Harley. They ate quietly. The only other thing that bothered them was the whispers that they had heard about the isles losing their powers from the other people in the tavern.

By the time they were done eating, the men were gone, and it was just them left. They sat until the lady returned to clear the table.

"Can I ask you something?" Sage asked her.

"Oh yes, you can," she replied.

"We heard those men speak of a person, a person stealing the magic of the Isles. Who is it that's doing this evil? Do you know?"

The lady gasped in fear. "You must never bring her up. She is never to be mentioned. I hope you understand, good stranger, that if you go around asking questions, you might bring ill luck to yourself?"

Sage frowned. She pulled two silver coins out of the bunch from her pocket that Atkin had given them as a parting gift and gave them to her. The woman smiled, thanked them, and went about her business.

"I don't think we'll find our way back anytime soon. These people don't want to say anything about what's happening," Harley complained.

"It's fine. We'll find out very soon enough. We should leave now though. At least find our way around or find somewhere we can rest before we carry on," Juniper said.

"You have a point. Come on," Sage said, standing up.

They walked out of the tavern together and through the market. They were still going when a young boy held unto Juniper's legs.

"Please, you must help. Mother is sick. Mother might be dying. If my mother dies, I am all alone. Please, I beg of you."

The three of them followed the young boy as he led them through the dirty part of the city to an old run-down shack. Inside, shivering so bad, was a woman wrapped in dirty clothing.

"Would you be able to get the physician to come here?" Harley asked.

"They would not come. I owe them and since I do not work, I am unable to pay. Please, you must help me."

Sage got closer to the woman, getting on her knees and brushing the dirty mangled hair from the woman's cheeks.

"You'll be fine. I promise," Sage whispered.

Sage placed her hand on the woman's forehead and for whatever reason, she closed her eyes and willed healing energy to flow from her to the woman.

Sage felt another hand on her own. She could feel the energy leave her and embrace the woman lying on the bed. It was when she felt a buzz around her that she opened her eyes. The woman's eyes were open as well and she was staring at Sage and Juniper with wide eyes.

"Mother!" the boy screamed as he ran into his mother's arms.

Sage looked at her hands. They still felt warm, and so did Junipers. Harley just watched them with his mouth wide open. He had never seen something like that happen before. Sage got up and helped Juniper get up as well.

"Thank you, kind strangers. I don't know what you did, but my mother and I are grateful to you," the child told them.

Sage dug her hands into her pocket and pulled out four gold coins. They really wouldn't need all that money anyway. She dropped it in the boy's palm and closed it.

They left a minute later, but not before the boy's mother could show how grateful she was to Sage. She gave her a gold band. Sage didn't understand why, but she didn't reject the gift either.

As they left the shack, the place began to take a different form. With every step, something changed, until they were no longer standing in the dirt but in a different place entirely.

"You must be wondering where you are!" a voice came.

Sage turned back in the direction of the shack. It wasn't there anymore, but the lady that had once been sick stood there, in the most beautiful silver gown Sage had ever seen.

"You passed your first test, Sage and Juniper. You showed kindness and empathy and helped a boy you were not sure was being honest. You tried to heal someone, even though you weren't sure if you could. I have given you a gift in return." She turned to her side and the little boy walked out from behind her. He was in princely attire now.

"Harley, you were kind and patient and wished me health. For that, accept this little token of mine. It will grant you strength at your weakest hour and protect you too. Go on now, go give it to him," she said to the little boy.

He ran to Harley with a golden band. Harley wore it on his left pinky finger. Juniper realized she now had a small tattoo on her wrist. An image of a dove.

"Sage, your gift will lead you on the right path. You'll come to understand. Remember, to be a witch is to love and be loved. To be a witch is to harm no one. To be a witch is following the moon. To be a witch is to be kind and caring. To be a witch is to live with nature. To be a witch is to grow and learn. Very soon, fear, anxiety, and doubt will be washed away by calming waves, to be replaced by success, abundance, and joy. The Universe has heard your calling, and it has been answered. You are so close now to realizing your destiny."

In the blink of an eye, they were back in the same place where they'd been standing, but the shack was gone. The gifts they had gotten still remained with them.

"Okay, whoa! I think we just met a goddess," Harley stated.

"I got to agree to that one. Sage, this is a much different thing from what I imagined a goddess would be. She's cool. The problem now is that we didn't ask her where to head from here. Got any clues?"

Chapter Seven

>) ● ((

Their first test had been to help a sick person. That was something Sage could easily do. It was something she wished everyone could do, help those in need as much as one could.

Sage wasn't sure what the second test would be. Though she was not afraid, she didn't know what to expect from everything that had happened so far.

It was dark now, so they had to look for a place to sleep. Sage could already feel her legs burning in her trainers. Lucky she had actually worn casual shoes for casual Friday. She wondered how Harley and Juniper were holding up too. She was a bit tired. They walked back to the market, in search of a guest house to sleep in. It would be hard to find one at such a time. The thought of sleeping out in the cold made Sage shiver. They turned a different corner and as they did, a woman in bohemian clothing grabbed hold of Sage's hand.

"Hey!" Sage yelled.

But the woman didn't stop. She dragged Sage while Juniper and Harley ran after her. She stopped at a small wooden shack, dimly lit with candles. The woman had incense burning too, and the place smelled like lavender. It reminded Sage of her house. Quiet, quaint, and homey.

"For what reason have you brought me here?" Sage asked her.

"Sit. Sit down. Your friends must be here anytime soon. Come now, sit down, child. Would you like some tea? I've got lavender and honey, a little bit of chamomile in it," the old lady said.

Sage looked shocked. She rubbed her wrist, hoping it wasn't bruised from the woman holding it too tight. *How does she know? Juniper and Grandmother are the only ones who know what kind of tea I love to drink,* Sage thought. She quietly sat down.

The woman poured them both a cup of tea. Sage took a deep breath, letting the aroma of lavender, honey, and chamomile fill her up. She took a sip and moaned from the taste of the tea on the tip of her tongue.

"You're on the right path, but something is missing," the old lady said.

Behind them, the curtains ruffled, and two different footsteps rushed into the shack.

"Ah, you're here now. Come sit. It's time for me to read the glass," the lady said.

Harley and Juniper looked at themselves and then joined Sage on the pile of pillows that were scattered across the room on the floor.

"Juniper. You're gifted, my child. You have within you healing energy. You thrive more in the peace and quiet of nature. And your soul is entwined with that of another who loves nature as much as you."

In a different scenario, maybe Juniper would have yelled excitedly. But at this point, only a few things now surprised her. Yes, she longed to see Ash, that was the only thing the old boho woman reminded her of.

"Harley. You find peace only in the eyes of the one whom you want. They're the missing part of your soul, taken from you long before you were formed. You searched for them and now you search no more. But you will find them. Their destiny and yours are interconnected in the most astounding manner. Your courage and strength belong to you. When you think all hope is lost, remember that you stand up every time you fall."

Harley was still getting used to this whole thing. He felt vulnerable, but not in a bad way. The bohemian woman was right anyway. He had been in search of one person for a long time. He had seen her in his dreams, a part of him being pulled away. Now that he'd found her, he wasn't so sure of himself anymore. Harley turned in time to catch Sage's eyes on him. Sage had a pale complexion that he really liked, and her dark brown hair fell in curly waves around her shoulders. He sometimes wondered how she was able to tame the beast every morning. Her lapis-colored eyes turned a dreamy blue color under certain lighting. It was that same dreamy blue color he was staring at now. But the woman broke their connection.

"Sage. Your life is filled with adventure. You mustn't give up. You've passed your first test; you will find that the next test is much more challenging. You do not have a connection with the one who brought you forth to the world. You must retrace your steps. To be able to do that, you must embrace your past and learn to forgive. In this next test, you must fight your battles alone. Alone, I tell you."

"What do you mean by retracing my steps? We've come so far already," Sage began to say.

But the bohemian woman had already stopped rubbing the glass ball with her hand. Sage knew she would not answer her anymore.

"I know you do not have a place to rest your head. I have a spare room. It might not give you comfort, but it will be enough for the night."

The bohemian lady led them to a room in the shack. It was big enough for the three of them. Harley laid down on the soft pillows and Sage joined him quietly.

"You know what I wouldn't mind doing now? Take a long bath. It would be wonderful to feel water running down my skin again," Juniper said before joining them on the makeshift bed.

"Yeah. I wouldn't mind having pizza right now or even cereal. I missed my early morning smoothie," Harley said.

In the dark, Sage found his hand and gave it a squeeze. He squeezed back and brought the hand to his lips, where he pressed a soft kiss there. Sage turned pink in the darkness.

Sage closed her eyes. Somehow, she stayed still and quiet. Slowly, she drifted into sleep. But then, her eyes were wide open again. This time, she was in the meadow filled with wildflowers once again. Why did she always find herself here? She started to walk through the field and as she did, she could hear the laughter of a child. A five-year-old child. She ran through the fields, petals sticking to her hair, and as she did, she twirled. Not too far from the child was a woman. She was making a painting, a painting of the little girl.

Sage got closer, and the girl saw her. Sage knew who the girl was. But she didn't say a word. Instead, she just stared at her.

"Do you like flowers too? I love flowers! They're my favorite!" the little girl said.

Sage recognized the voice, the laughter, the doll hanging from her right hand. She recognized the pajamas, and more than anything, she recognized the child. She recognized herself.

"Baby? Who is there? Who are you talking to?"

Her mother's voice. Sage turned to look at her. She had dropped her paint brush and was now running towards them.

"Hello, there," Sage said the minute her mother got closer. "I promise, I mean no harm."

Her mother grabbed her little hand and pulled her behind her small frame. Sage watched as she peeked from behind her mother's skirt.

"How did you get here? Who are you?" her mother asked again. "Are you here to hurt us?"

"I'm not here to hurt you. I honestly do not know how I got here either. One minute I was in bed and the next, I was here," Sage answered. "I really mean you no harm. I came in search of my mother. She abandoned me years ago."

Sage watched her mother's eyes go from fear to worry, then surprise.

"Oh, you poor thing. Come sit with us for a few minutes," she said. "Sage, would it be alright to share some of your cakes and fruits with the nice lady?"

Little Sage gave a firm nod and then ran off to grab the cakes and fruits where her mother had left them.

Her mother led her to the blanket she had spread out hours before she started painting. She sat down on the blanket and ushered Sage to join her.

"Poor child. I wonder why your mother would do such a thing to you. Every time I think of losing my little Sage, I feel my heart squeeze so hard that I can't breathe. But then, your mother must have had her reasons, you know. I don't know what they are, but I hope you find it in your heart to forgive her someday. Would you like some tea? My little birdie made it this morning. We kept it in a flask, so it is still hot."

Sage's mother had always been like this, quick to lose focus. But she never forgot if something was on her mind.

Her mother poured the tea into a mug and handed it to her. The aroma of lavender hit her hard. Little Sage offered her cakes as well. Sage took a bite of the cake. She chewed slowly, reveling in the taste of the cake. Then she took a sip of the tea.

Sage took a deep breath as a single teardrop rolled down her cheeks. Her mother didn't seem to notice, but little Sage did. She got up and wiped the tear, then she placed a soft kiss on her forehead.

"It's going to be alright, Gramma says when I cry. Do you want more kisses?" she asked.

"I'm alright now," Sage replied.

"Okay! I'll go play in the flowers."

Sage watched her leave. She noticed her mother staring at her. She wondered if she had recognized her now. But the look her mother gave her was not one of familiarity. No. It was something else. It was warm and filled with love.

"I feel like I know you. That I've seen you. What is your name?"

"I'm named after a plant," Sage replied, knowing it would cause her mother to start talking about her name. It was something she learned as a child. In order to get out of a punishment, Sage would ask a trick question, just the way her grandmother taught her, and then her mother would answer it and forget what it was that she was to punish Sage about.

"Yes. My Sage is named after a plant. They have these beautiful flowers that are almost purplish in color. Do you know…"

Sage watched her mother talk for a few minutes about her name. The urge to lay her head down on her mother's lap was so strong that she found herself doing it. Absentmindedly, her mother stroked her hair. She hummed a soft tune as she pulled her fingers through Sage's locks.

"Do you know why I called you Sage?" she asked.

Sage knew her mother wasn't talking directly to her, so she stayed on her lap quietly.

"Because your father brought me a sage flower the day you were born. He loved the plant and I loved him and together, we showered all that love on you."

Sage silently cried on her mother's lap. She overflowed with her mother's love. Why did she blame her for everything that had happened? It wasn't her fault at all. Was this what the bohemian woman was trying to warn her about? Sage felt a hand wipe her eyes as her mother began to sing quietly.

When she was still very little, her mother would sing this spell over and over again. She told Sage that if she were ever to get lost, she should sing it and it would guide her back home.

Home! That was it. The spell could probably take them home. Wasn't that the reason why she was brought to her past?

But the song only put her to sleep. Sage closed her eyes and began to drift into sleep. It started slowly until exhaustion took absolute control of her weakness and she gave in to slumber.

When Sage opened her eyes again, Harley was holding her close to himself and rocking her back and forth. It was only then Sage realized she had been crying in her sleep.

"Shush, it's alright now. Nothing can hurt you here. You're safe here now. Nothing can hurt you now, Sage. Please wake up."

The room materialized in Sage's eyes as she opened them. It was still dark inside, but she could see a flicker of light from outside.

Harley let her go slowly. Beside her, Juniper was still fast asleep. Sage was grateful that her crying hadn't woken her up.

"Thank you, Harley," she whispered.

"It's alright, Sage. You kept calling for your mother and I know it's a touchy subject for you. I got worried and just decided to comfort you. Do you still want to get back to sleep?"

"Thanks, Harley. I think I'll stay up. There's really no need to go back to bed," Sage replied.

"I'm also awake. Do you want to talk about it? About your mum, I mean."

"Okay. What do you want to know?" Sage asked him.

"What's your favorite thing about her? What caused you both to get separated?" he asked.

Sage wanted to shrug like she usually did, but instead, she sat up and pulled her legs together so she could place her chin on her knees.

"My mother was this awesome person to me as a child. She wasn't perfect, but she knew magic tricks that I was never tired of seeing. She had a lot of flaws, but now I don't blame her for any of that either. My mother left me at my grandma's house. Often, I would spend a couple of days there, but she would always be back to fetch me. We fought most of the time and at six years old, we had our biggest fight. My mother got frustrated with me. She put me in the car and drove all the way to my grandmother's house. She dropped me at the door and then got in a fight with my grandma as well.

"It was a really big fight this time. My grandmother said some nasty things to my mother and my mother returned some of hers too. I couldn't understand why. My mother placed a sad kiss on my forehead before she left. That was the last time I saw her. I watched her speed away from my grandmother's cottage."

Harley sighed. "I see why you resent her so much. She did you wrong."

"I thought she would come back, at least to visit. Every night I would stand outside in my pajamas, and she wouldn't show up. Do you want to know the last time I saw her? My grandmother's funeral. She stayed for a few days. Every night, she would slip a black tourmaline or a clear quartz into my room, until the funeral was done. She left two days later, unable to handle my drama."

"I'm sorry about everything you've been through. Your grandma is a ten out of ten though, for making sure you were okay all those years. But then, the pain within you won't leave if you don't let it go. You need to forgive your mum. She did do wrong, but the more you hold unto that pain, the more it will grow into something else. Remember what the nice old lady said? You must learn to forgive, Sage."

Sage looked at Harley. There was nothing more that she wanted to do at the moment other than kiss him. Afraid of how he would take it, she instead pulled him into a tight hug. Harley hugged her right back.

"Thank you, Harley."

"What for?" Harley asked, still holding her.

"For listening. Juniper is the only person who knows about this. My group of friends don't know, so that makes you the second person who knows."

"Hold on one second, did you say a group of friends?" Harley asked, breaking away.

"Yeah, I just did. Why?" Sage asked him.

"You have a group of friends? Really? I thought that aside from Juniper, you didn't talk to anybody else."

"Don't you think that would be weird? I have friends close by and also scattered across the country. We try to catch up on each other's lives as much as we can."

"I'm honestly sorry. I thought you didn't like having friends. So I assumed Juniper was your only friend."

"Hey, but you're my friend now, you know. I don't just tell anyone things about myself. It's fine, honestly. My friends are just the same as I am. The only difference is, they don't go on adventures like this with me."

Harley laughed and Sage listened. She had a feeling that Juniper was awake but wasn't saying anything. She was grateful for that.

"Do you think we will get out of here?" Harley asked quietly.

"I know we will. I'm certain we will. The old lady said only I know the way, so I'll figure it out."

Harley pulled her in for another hug before letting her go once more. He laid on the makeshift bed, but Sage stayed up for the rest of the night. They would leave this place, no matter how long it might take.

Chapter Eight

)) ● ((

The next morning, the bohemian lady gave them food. Sage offered to pay her, but the old lady would not take it. When it was time for them to leave, she pulled Sage aside.

"You left last night, and you paid your past a visit. Do you remember now? I'll take you and your friends to the field. There, you must try again and again until you eventually figure it out. Do you understand child?"

"Your words are often confusing. Do you know that?" Sage asked her.

"Of course, I do. Your mother used to hum you a song. She said it would lead you back home. It will. Now, follow me."

Sage said nothing, but she followed the older boho woman and so did her friends. She took them through fields until they were out in the middle of nowhere.

It looked identical to the field where Sage and her mother once used to cut flowers. But this time, it wasn't a flower field or a meadow. It was empty. When they turned to thank the bohemian lady, she was gone. Nowhere to be seen.

"One thing is certain, if that lady wanted us dead, we would all be dead," Harley said.

Sage and Juniper chuckled.

"Do you think there's some sort of portal here?" Juniper asked Sage.

"No. I think we're supposed to find our way out of the Isle of Man," answered Sage. "The boho lady insists I must remember a spell my mother always hummed to me whenever we were out picking flowers."

"You don't remember? You were humming a song in your sleep last night," Harley said.

"I don't remember it at all, Harley. I wish I did," Sage replied. She remembered humming the song alongside her mother, but she didn't sing it out loud. Sage sat on the bare ground and made a wide circle. Underneath her hand, the circle grew hot. Sage withdrew her hand once she felt it.

"Hey, are you okay?" Juniper asked.

"It's nothing. I've got it under control. Don't worry," Sage replied.

Sage sat in the middle of the circle monk style and then closed her eyes. She took a long deep breath and imagined herself back in the meadow with her mother. When Sage opened her eyes, she was back in the meadow again. This time, her mother was there, alone.

"You're here," Sage said as she got closer. Her mother dropped the paint brush. This time she wasn't making a painting of little Sage.

"Who are you?" her mother asked, confused.

Sage looked at the painting. It was the same one hanging in her grandmother's room back home.

"You're making a painting. Something feels missing from it, you know? Something that's supposed to be right there?" Sage pointed at the center, where she would always be in her mother's paintings.

"I know what you mean. It is I who feels it the most. The pain of losing something. Would you like to know why it is empty?" her mother asked her.

Sage stood next to her. "Yes please," she whispered.

"I loved her father so much that I left a part of me with him. And then she reminded me so much of the part of me that I left with him that I had to leave her too. It hurts, but it is for her own good. We have to make sacrifices for the people we love, don't we?" her mother said.

"Do you miss her?" Sage asked.

"Every day since I left her, yes. Yes, I do. I want her back here with me, but it will only give us both so much pain. I only want what's best for her. I hope she forgives me someday. I hope she knows that her mother loves her so much."

Her mother crumbled to the ground and began to sob. Sage knew there was only one way to calm her, so she began to hum the spell. She tried to recall her mother reciting it as they picked flowers with which to decorate a crown. It had been ages since she'd heard the spell. But as she hummed it softly, her mother began to recite it herself.

"From ancient times long past. Help me leave this vast land. Take me to a place where the flowers grow. Take me to where my ancestors sow. The seeds of new, a sky so blue, take me now through the heavens to you."

Sage pulled her into a hug as waves and waves of emotions hit her. She wiped her own tears and cupped her mother's cheeks with both her hands.

"I forgive you, Mum."

The bright light that enveloped the two of them sent Sage right back into her body. She took a long deep breath and opened her eyes. Juniper and Harley were looking at her.

"Do you know you scared us?" they both shouted simultaneously.

"Oh, goodness. My ears! It feels like you both turned into one big Juniper. My eardrums hurt now!"

"Well then, don't scare us like that again. Harley thought you were dead," Juniper said, slightly amused.

"In my defense, she wasn't moving. And you were about to start crying too, weren't you?" Harley said, his eyes twinkling with mischievousness.

"Okay. That's enough between you two. You aren't little kids anymore. You're both grown adults."

"Did you hear that, Juniper? You're an old woman now, act your age!" Harley stuck his tongue out at her.

"Says the man who would give anything to have a slice of pizza."

They were still bickering minutes later as Sage drew a new circle large enough for three people to stand in. She stood in it for a few minutes before deciding to break Juniper and Harley apart.

"I forgave my mum," she said.

Juniper stopped to look at her. "You did what now?"

"I forgave her. I retraced my steps, embraced my past and forgave my mother," Sage said.

"I'm just going to say that I didn't expect that," Harley stated. He brushed his hair back.

"At least that stopped the teenage bickering. Now get in the circle. We don't have much time left. If the spell leaves my memory, I might have to astral project and two adults might start thinking I'm dead, if I do."

"Astral projection! That's the gift that was given to you, right? That's a cool gift," Juniper said.

She stepped inside the circle and so did Harley. Sage took both their hands and held on tightly. They did the same.

"This might not take us home, but it will take us where we need to be. That's what's more important right now. It isn't going home; it's figuring out how to fix the problem this magical dimension has. And we won't be able to leave until we figure it out. Are you guys with me?"

"We are."

That was enough for Sage. She began to hum the spell first, before saying it out loud.

"From ancient times long past. Help me leave this vast land. Take me to a place where the flowers grow. Take me to where my ancestors sow. The seeds of new, a sky so blue, take me now through the heavens to you."

She repeated the spell until a bright light engulfed them completely. Sage held on tight to Juniper and Harley, refusing to let go.

"Mmhf. Not again!" Sage groaned as she tried to get the leg blocking her airway off her body. Once she was successful, she sat up, trying to breathe in as much air as possible.

Sage opened her eyes. The sights before her were magnificent. She said nothing, but her mouth hung open and her eyes were wide in surprise.

The spell didn't take them home as expected. It took them somewhere else. It took them to a land weirder and more beautiful. How did she not come to know a place like this existed? The sky looked like it had the texture of cotton candy and so did the clouds. The creatures had features similar to that of butterflies, but they were humongous. They had horns shaped like that of a unicorn and their backs were arched in a manner that showed they could be ridden. Sage tapped Harley and Juniper until they both groaned. Certain they were starting to wake, Sage got up. She took off her shoes and felt the texture of the grass. It was the softest she had ever stood on. It seemed to melt underneath her feet. She sat back on the ground and pressed her palm on the grass. It was the same thing.

The air smelled sweet, like candy floss. There were gems and crystals of different kinds and colors everywhere she looked. Some creatures were florescent and others transparent.

"Oh my! Where are we now?" Juniper asked, coming to stand beside Sage.

"Grandma didn't tell me about this place. Believe me, I don't know where we are. It's so beautiful. I feel like if I blink, it might go away."

Harley joined them seconds later, and he was just as mesmerized as they were. He had never seen anything like it before. His mouth hung open for a second.

"Okay, is anyone going to tell me why it feels like I'm in a movie?" Harley asked.

"Believe me, if I knew the answer, I'd have given it long ago," Sage answered.

The plants were humongous. They had different colors. Some had multiple layers and others were wide enough for anyone to shelter under. There were birds as well, with wingspans that made Sage, Juniper, and Harley think they were back in the time of dinosaurs.

"I promise, this looks just like a movie scene. Like something we've seen before. Look at all the vibrant colors here!" Harley said.

They walked down the path, with Sage leading the way. Something hopped in front of her, a lilac bunny with wings.

"Okay, this is way more than I expected. There's a bunny with wings here!"

Sage knelt down in front of the little bunny. It sniffed her face. Sage brought her hand close. The bunny sniffed her hand before moving and nuzzled into Sage's palm. She brushed the bunny's fur. It was so soft that she groaned happily.

"I don't think I've felt anything as soft as its fur. I wish I had something to give it. Come here and feel it yourself."

When the bunny had gotten enough attention, it flew away. They continued walking, even though they weren't sure where they were heading. They came across a huge waterfall with sparkling luminescent colors. The water was quiet, there was absolutely no sound as it dropped down into a pool of water below.

"I could live here forever," Juniper said, "but not without my babies," she added.

Sage had to agree. The place was quiet and beautiful, ethereal. The kind of place that Sage would want to live in forever.

They walked past the waterfall and into a wide expanse of land. What looked like it was supposed to be a city was floating in the clouds, with translucent bridges. The clouds looked like candy floss—pink, blue, and light green colors were scattered everywhere.

Harley grabbed Sage's hand and brought it to his chest.

"Where have you brought us, Sage? It's the most beautiful place I've ever seen."

"You can say that again, Harley," Juniper stated.

Sage chuckled. "There's so much magic here. Pure, untainted magic. The kind that brings you peace."

"Your bracelet is glowing, Sage." Harley dropped Sage's hand.

Sage looked at it. The bracelet was made from pure white magic. Sage turned to look at Juniper's wrist. Her dove tattoo was glowing as well and so was Harley's golden band.

Her bracelet thrummed with life. Sage took it off and placed it on the ground. It levitated and then turned east. They ran after it. Harley ran ahead of them. Sage and Juniper were not exactly made for running, but they tried their best. They continued to run for a few more minutes before the bracelet paused. It hung in midair for a few minutes before dropping onto the ground. It stopped glowing. Sage drew closer. At first, she was afraid. She didn't know what to expect.

She grabbed the gold chain. As she did, her fingers brushed something solid. Sage jumped back in fear. Something started to crack. It started with just one line, then more lines, until the shield was completely destroyed. Sage looked at what stood in front of her in surprise.

Three women looked back at her. One was around her grandmother's age, while the other two looked a bit younger than the first one. Sage was still taking everything in when two sets of eyes joined the other three.

"Ah, you arrived sooner than we expected," the older woman said, then she turned to one of the young women. "You could have warned us about the shield. It will take another two full moons to rebuild it this strong."

"Look here, she touched it only once and it fell apart completely? That never happened before, Mother," the second young lady replied, looking at the space that once used to be where the shield stood.

"That's alright. She's very powerful, you see. She doesn't quite know that yet," the older lady stated.

"I'm sorry to intrude, but you do know we're right in front of you, yes?" Sage asked.

"Ah, yes. We do. Now come on in. Lira made tea. Let's hope we don't turn blue this time," the older lady said with a smile.

"Should my friends and I be worried about turning blue?" Sage asked.

"You don't have to worry," the one Sage assumed was Lira said. "I only made a slight mistake. It's been one full circle already and they haven't let it go. I think you all should worry about weaving the shield. If dear old Mr. Bartly comes around, he might not leave for two circles. And remember, he doesn't need an invitation anymore because someone else gave him a lifetime of that."

All the women, both young and old began to grumble. Sage wondered who this Mr. Bartly was, but it wasn't in her place to ask questions.

"Come sit. You must be tired. That was a long journey. My name is Rekha, and these women are my children and grandchildren. There's Frieda and Tala, there's Ambrosia and Rose, and Crystal and Lira."

The problem with this was, Rekha had only called their names without pointing out who was who exactly.

"It's great to meet all of you. These are my friends Harley and Juniper. I am Sage," Sage said, doing the same thing.

The cup of tea poured its contents into the cups. Each cup floated to someone. When the cup levitated towards Sage, she held it and waited for the women to take a sip of their tea first. Harley and Juniper followed her lead.

They did almost at the same time and at the same time, they all spat it out.

"Lira, what did you do this time around?" Rekha asked. "The tea tastes like a wet sock soaked in salty water."

"I wouldn't know. I followed the recipe you gave me," Lira protested.

"And what is the recipe?" the woman who Lira looked like asked.

"The sock in tea recipe," Lira said proudly.

All the women palmed their foreheads at the same time, then groaned in frustration and giggled.

Chapter Nine

))●((

The women were extra nice. Rekha reminded Sage of her grandmother, with her long gray locks and her green-colored eyes. She smiled all the time, even when Lira did something wrong. It was obvious she was the youngest. She looked to be fifteen or sixteen. She was carefree.

Frieda and Tala were twins. Frieda was the mother to Ambrosia and Rose, twins as well, while Crystal and Lira belonged to Tala. The problem now, was this: you couldn't tell the twins apart. Even their mother could not tell them apart.

"You'll need to take a bath, all three of you. A cleansing bath. I don't think you've touched clean water in the last couple of days. I'm aware. Ambrosia and Crystal will prepare baths for you. Then, you can join us for dinner."

"Finally!" Harley groaned.

All the women turned to him. When Harley saw the number of eyes looking at him, he blushed, visibly embarrassed.

The women led Sage to the bath house where a hot bath was waiting for her. There was as much bath salts and oils as she could possibly need, and she could smell the scent of lavender.

They took her sweatshirt, jeans, and her underwear. In place of that, they left a silk gown. Sage took time scrubbing herself. She had missed having her cleansing bath. Now that she could finally have one, she wanted to make sure she got every bit of dirt off her skin. She continuously scrubbed every inch of skin on her body before dipping herself in the bathtub. She washed her hair as well, getting out all the dirt from it.

By the time she was out of the bathtub, her skin smelled like lavender and honey, just how she liked it. Sage brushed her hair while it was wet because it was the only way to brush it easily. Then she pulled it into a ponytail and left it that way. She wore the gown the women had left for her. The cloth adjusted itself to fit her. Satisfied with how she looked, Sage left the bath house.

"Feeling great?" Juniper asked the moment she saw her.

"Yes, I am. Do you know how good it is to have clean hair and freshly cleaned skin?" Sage asked her in return.

"It feels good," Harley said.

He was wearing an old pair of pants that Sage was certain must have belonged to Rekha in her youth.

"You laugh at me, and I'll ask one of them to do something about it," Harley said.

"You know you can get the pants to magically suit you, right?" Juniper asked Harley.

"How?"

"Use your imagination, Harley," Juniper replied.

At first, Harley was skeptical, but once he thought of it, the pants changed form to suit him perfectly. So did the shirt that he had been given.

"So, we can't do anything about the shoes?" Harley asked.

"No, we can't. They have a doormat. Now come on. We need to know more about where we are."

They both followed Sage into the house. The aroma of perfectly baked pie hit them in the face. Harley licked his lips.

"Oh, you're all here. Come join us at the table. The food is ready," Rekha said, leading them to the long dining table.

"But it's bright outside. It's almost like daytime. How do you know when it's time for dinner?" Harley asked.

"If you haven't noticed already, child, you're on the Isle of the Three Moons. Unlike the other isles that you have previously been to, our magic is stronger. Everything thrives on magic here. You must have walked past the crystal city on your way here, yes?"

"Yes," all three of them answered.

"The crystal city, its creatures, and everything else is built on pure magic. The guardians of the oracle rule over it."

"The oracle?" Sage asked.

"Yes, Sage," Rekha continued. "When you chanted the spell that brought you here, a door opened. A portal door. It brought you straight to our dimension. In order to leave, you must first seek the oracle."

Just like the tea had poured itself from the kettle, the food dished itself. Sage, Juniper, and Harley dug in without waiting for their hosts to begin eating. They were that hungry. Traveling from one dimension to another was very exhausting and energy consuming. It left them tired and hungry. Sage shoveled spoonful after spoonful of food into her mouth. When it was time for dessert, Harley's mouth watered at the sight of the pie.

After dinner, Sage was sure she couldn't move from the spot where she was sitting at the dining table. But she was able to walk to a soft looking couch in the women's sitting room.

"Full?" Juniper asked her.

"I think I ate way too much."

"Me too," Harley added.

The women let them be and it wasn't long until they were all asleep.

"How long were we asleep?" Sage asked Rekha.

They were outside now, trying to weave the shield back into place. Sage didn't know how to help, so she sat back and watched.

"Throughout the night. You found your clothes," Rekha stated.

Sage stared at her clean sweatshirt and jeans. Her sneakers were clean as well. She had woken up on a bed, next to Juniper. Her clothes were sitting at the foot of the bed they were lying on.

"Yes. I wanted to say thank you for your hospitality, Rekha. But I'm certain you know why we've traveled so far. Can you tell me?"

"When your friends are awake, I will. Now go have breakfast. The twins must be done by now."

The aroma of the food must have woken Juniper and Harley because they were already at the table, eating porridge with freshly baked bread. Sage joined them, but she tried not to eat too much.

The women led them far from their quaint cottage, leaving behind the quiet twins to weave the shield. They led them through fields of flowers until they arrived at a hill. At the top of the hill was a cave.

The cave seemed old. The opening of the cave was sealed with a rock. Rekha walked toward what would have been the entrance of the cave if it hadn't been sealed.

Whatever was inside the cave called out to Sage. It thrummed with energy and so did Sage's gold bracelet. Rekha took off a chain that had been hidden from sight before now and placed it on the seal. The rock shook and vibrated, the ground beneath it opened and the rock that had been sealing the entrance to the cave slide down into the ground.

"Welcome," said Rekha, "to the Crystal cave."

Harley was the first to cross the threshold. When nothing happened to him, Sage and Juniper joined him as well.

The crystals in the cave vibrated with so much energy that Sage thought they would explode. She had never seen a place like this before. There were different crystals, some that she didn't even know. Sage was amazed. She felt at peace with the cave. The powerful colors of the crystals were blinding in some spots. She could also see some of her favorites—indigo, vibrant greens, and blues bringing clarity, healing, balance, and wisdom. They could feel their inner strength come alive, a newfound confidence and warmth. The minerals were rich with power. It's like they could feel the energy flowing through their chakra system. Sage could see lapis lazuli, a deep blue with white streaks. The biggest celestite crystal she had ever seen. Some with rich fluorite minerals flowing through. The list was endless. It felt like heaven.

"The oracle awaits you. It will guide you, just as the Universe guides your steps. Go now. We'll be right out here, waiting for you." Sage was still in a dream, overwhelmed with the pulsating vibrations of the giant crystals.

"But what are we supposed to do in there?" Sage asked Rekha.

"You will know when you get there," Rekha replied to her.

The cave was quiet. Sage led the way, deeper and deeper into the cave. Juniper and Harley followed quietly. The only sounds that they could hear were the sounds of their own feet touching the polished crystalized floor of the cave. Sage continued to walk until they arrived in a room the size of a hall. Every part of the room was covered in crystals. Crystals so clear, Sage could see her reflection.

At the center of the hall, were four little pillars that stood an inch lower than Sage's height. On it was a book. But as Sage tried to step closer, an invisible force stopped her.

"Stand where you are, child, unless you seek destruction!"

The voice echoed through the hall. Sage stepped back and Harley took a protective stand before her and Juniper.

"Who are you? And why have you asked us to come here?" Sage said.

The voice chuckled, the laughter bouncing off the walls of the hall. When it became silent again, a figure in a robe appeared next to the pillar. Sage tried hard to see who it was, but all she could see was darkness underneath the hood.

"I am the oracle. Formed long ago. Guardian of the multiverse and protector of the divine. You, my child, have come in search of something. You seek that which belongs to me. Do you not, child?" The oracle asked.

Sage stood as tall as she could. "We only have questions. We wish to go back home."

"And you must have witnessed how impossible that is, by now. You still wish to try? Your job is not yet complete, child. There is much to be done. Much to be done."

"Why have we been brought here? We're just ordinary people trying to live our lives," Harley said.

"Ordinary? Ordinary, you say? Everything you have done up until this moment has been more than ordinary. It has been extraordinary, boy. This is your next quest. The crystal book is given only to those with the purest of hearts, but to have it, you must will it to come to you."

"How?" Juniper asked.

"Juniper. Quiet and understanding. If your heart is pure, call out to the book and it will come to you. But you must be strong-willed in order to do so."

104

With a loud belly rumbling laughter, the oracle was gone. Sage turned to Harley and Juniper.

"We came this far; we can at least try to get the crystal book. It might have answers to our questions," Sage suggested.

"I agree," Juniper said. "Trying won't harm any of us."

"If you both agree, who am I to argue? Let's give it a shot."

Harley took Sage's hand and Sage took Juniper's hand. Together, they took deep breaths as Sage began to chant a spell.

"If my heart be as pure as the crystals, I summon thee, book of spells, return to me," Sage began.

Juniper and Harley joined in the chant, their voices blending to become one. At first it seemed like nothing different had happened. But Sage continued to chant, and Juniper and Harley didn't stop either. The energy that gradually surrounded them began to grow with every passing second.

The more they chanted, the more the energy grew. A light so bright enveloped them. Sage felt the book moving toward them, but she didn't stop chanting. When she opened her eyes, the crystal book of spells was levitating in front of them. It hovered continuously until Sage stretched her hand to receive the book. It dropped into her hand, and she caught it.

The book was large and bound with leather. It had three beautiful crystals on the front cover of the book. And all three crystals were shaped like crescent moons. Sage opened the book, brushing the intricately carved patterns on it with her hands.

"Indeed, you're divine. Your quest does not stop here. The book now belongs to you, its rightful owners, but you must use it only for good. The day you should do otherwise, it'll come back here, where it will always belong. To summon the book, you must chant the spell. It will leave when its job is done. You must go now. Your last challenge awaits you at the Isle of Darkness ! May your journey lead to success."

Sage, Juniper, and Harley found themselves back at the entrance of the cave. The book was nowhere to be seen, but Rekha and her granddaughters were patiently waiting.

"Did you get it?" Rekha asked the minute she saw them.

"If you mean to ask if we passed the test, the answer is yes. We did. We're to move on to our next quest," Harley answered.

"Wow, it's been years since anyone has been able to get the book," Rekha said.

"As much as we would love to come back with you to the cottage and eat all the nice pies your daughters make, we have to go. Our journey hasn't come to an end," Sage said.

Rekha smiled, trying to hide her disappointment. She pulled Sage into a hug, then Juniper and Harley.

"Promise you'll visit again?" she asked.

"After we succeed in our quest, we will come to visit."

The good witches followed them down the hill to the fields. There, they bid them goodbye. Sage drew a circle on a clear opening in the field. When she was done, Juniper and Harley stepped into the circle. Hands held tightly together, they began to chant the spell.

"From ancient times long past. Help me leave this vast land. Take me to a place where the flowers grow. Take me to where my ancestors sow. The seeds of new, a sky so blue, take me now through the heavens to you."

The bright light enveloped them again. This time it was stronger. The portal doors opened faster than before. Realizing that they were stronger than they were the last time they went through the portal, they walked through unafraid of whatever it was that would be waiting on the other side.

Chapter Ten

))●((

"Baby?" Sage's grandmother called out to her.

"Yes, Grandma!" Sage answered, running to the kitchen with her doll.

"I hope you know that just as much as there are good people on earth and in the Universe, there are bad people as well. Sometimes the good people have some evil in them and sometimes the evil people have some good in them. Do you understand me?"

"Not really, Gramma. Why would evil people have good in them? Aren't they just bad people?" Sage asked.

"Sometimes, we think people are evil of their own accord and we judge them, but that is far from the truth, my child. As you grow older, you will come to understand that most evil people were, at some point in life, filled with kindness and love."

"Is my mummy evil for leaving me here and not coming back because I got a little too curious and asked a lot of questions, Grams?"

"No, little birdie," her grandmother said.

The name caused so much emotion, but more than anything, it caused her pain.

"I'm not a little birdie anymore, Gramma. Please don't call me that?"

"Sure thing, Sagey. I won't call you little birdie anymore. But I will tell you this, just like I always have. Your mummy left for a reason. She never abandoned you. There are just too many things in her past that she wants to run away from."

"So she left me behind. She could have taken me with her. We could have run away together."

Her grandmother stared at her. She wasn't so tall, and she still dragged her doll around with her. She hadn't stopped wearing her pajamas either.

"Your mummy might come back someday. She left the most precious jewel in the world with the two of us."

"And what is that?"

"She left you with me. And she left you her heart."

Her grandmother placed a small kiss on her forehead before turning back to put the cookies in the oven.

"Don't forget, Sagey. Evil thrives in darkness, but love and kindness thrive where there is light."

The portal door opened to a new realm. The moment they arrived; a cold shiver ran down Sage's spine. She didn't like the energy in the place. It was too negative. She could feel hate, envy, jealousy, anger, frustration, and more than anything, she could feel fear. So much crippling fear.

It almost threw her off balance. Sage looked up to the sky. There was no light at all. She couldn't tell if it was night or daytime. The only source of light was so dim that it didn't seem like light at all.

"Am I the only one who feels like they should bolt from this place?" Juniper asked.

"It isn't just you. I feel the same way too," Harley stated.

"The place is filed with evil. Its very core is dying out. Soon, it will cease to exist. I think we were sent here to figure out a way to help it thrive," Sage said.

"And how are we supposed to do that? We can't even find our way," Juniper protested.

"I'm not sure, Juni. Something in me says the very foundation of this isle isn't far away. We just have to feed it with enough light. I think it's nighttime. We'll have to rest somewhere. My bracelet will guide us."

Sage took off her bracelet. It glowed a gloomy red as it levitated in front of her. Even if the bracelet was to lead them to safety, they still needed light to find their way around.

Sage closed her eyes and concentrated on bringing forth light from within her. She felt the tips of her finger surge with energy. When she opened her eyes, a big ball of light was on her palm.

The bracelet glowed brighter and began to levitate toward the north. Sage, Harley, and Juniper followed it. They could only see the path that the light created for them, but not the rest of the thick darkness. The bracelet stopped in front of a door.

Sage knocked on the door three times. They waited for a few minutes before someone opened the door. Sage could not see their face, but a figure in the shape of a man stood there.

"Who is it that knocks at this hour?" a booming voice said.

"It is I, Sage, daughter of the divine. I am here with my friends. We mean no harm. We only seek refuge for the night," Sage answered.

When Sage brought the light closer to the man's face, he shrunk backward, refusing to face the light. He opened the door fully but avoided the light as much as he could.

The house was cold and dark. The man led all three of them up the stairs in the house until they stopped at a room. He opened the door for them to go in but refused to join them inside the room.

"There's a bell on the bedside table. Should you need anything at all, be sure to ring it."

"Thank you," Harley said. "We'll let you know if we are in need of anything."

The man shut the door so hard that Sage was afraid it would fall down. It didn't. The room was eerily cold and quiet. But so was the rest of the house. Everything about the place was off, but it was the only available place.

"There are three beds. I'll take the one in the middle," Sage said, sitting on the bed already.

"I'll take the one to your right," Harley said.

Juniper just shrugged and sat on the bed by the left side. She took off her shoes and got under the cold covers. Once again, she felt a cold shiver run down her spine.

In the middle of the night, they woke to hear a sound in the hall. Tendrils crawled through the doors and walls of the house, dark energy, one unlike anything Sage had ever seen before now. It wrapped itself around Harley first, but his ring glowed in the darkness and a full body armor suddenly covered him. The tendrils recoiled, appalled by the burning sensation it got from Harley. It went for Juniper next, but as it brushed her skin, it turned into beautiful white smoke, disappearing into the darkness. The tendrils recoiled once more.

It had nearly given up, but the energy from the one in the middle seemed to call out to it. It sniffed first, finding no form of protection. Nothing to keep it from penetrating her mind and corrupting her soul.

It went in through her nostrils, clouding her mind completely. Sage's body fought with it for a few short seconds before she let it take complete control. Now that it controlled her mind and body, it was time to empty her body of her soul.

Sage got up, quietly removing the sheets. She didn't put on any shoes either. She walked straight to the door and opened it.

She walked down the hall and down the stairs until she got to the door. She opened it and continued to walk.

Where am I? Why can't I access my body? Sage thought.

Your consciousness is present, but you have no control of your mind and body. Just your soul.

Eli! You're here? How come I can't hear myself? I'm saying something, but my mouth isn't moving! I can't move anything at all.

There's no need to be afraid, Sage. You're presently in the Isle of Darkness. The dark light seekers and negative energy seekers have taken all the light from this isle. It was once filled with life, love, hope, and peace. Now it is the most corrupt of all the isles.

What happened to it?

There were two brothers who ruled the isle. They were the perfect balance of good and evil. The good kept the evil at bay. But years and years ago, an enchantress arrived here, in search of some dark powers. The good brother could not sacrifice his evil brother, because he loved him too much. So he sacrificed himself. The enchantress, knowing she had won, sucked out the life force from the good brother, leaving the evil brother in charge. With the light bearer of the isle gone, darkness and evil thrived greatly.

So why am I here? Sage asked.

Only you can bring light back to this isle. You must find the heart of the isle. In it, you will find the brother whose life force has been stolen from him. You must infuse a little of your life force into him. He will return balance to his land. And he will grant you entrance to the enchantress' lands.

Is that so, Eli?

Trust the Universe, Sage. Everything falls into place at the right time.

Sage walked through the dark and corrupted castle. Fear, hate, frustration, envy, and jealousy filled her. It pumped through her veins.

The creatures made from darkness snarled and snapped their jaws at her, but she kept walking until she was in the throne room of the dark castle.

In the middle of the throne room, a heart beat slowly, softly. Sage stretched her hands to grab the heart, but something held her back. She tried and tried again, but the hands did not move.

Slowly, a bright light started from within her, burning the dark tendrils with it as it completely enveloped her. The light from within Sage exploded in the room, destroying every bit of darkness hiding within its walls. It caused the cocoon hiding the faint beating heart to explode as well. Sage took it in her hand and with every bit of energy she had left, she willed it into the heart.

Sage opened her eyes to see a bright light envelop the heart. It began to beat rapidly before exploding into a big bright light.

In the middle of the commotion was a man. His hair fell in waves, and he looked too ethereal to be human. He looked at his hands, before feeling his face, and then the rest of his body.

"I'm present. I exist once again. I'm alive. My land is in pain. My people are in pain."

He turned to face Sage. He studied her for a minute before moving toward her. As he did, an armor suddenly covered every inch of his bare body. He was levitating at first, but the minute he reached Sage, he brought his feet to the ground for the first time. With each step, energy pulsed through him and into the castle.

"Who are you?" he asked Sage. "How did you get on my isle? How did you get into my castle?"

Sage took a step back. How were you supposed to explain to a king imprisoned in his own castle that his brother had filled his lands with darkness? That he had consumed the light until there was nothing left of the light in the land?

"My name is Sage. Daughter of the light. I was led here by darkness so I could save the light," Sage replied.

"I do not know you, child," the king replied.

Sage smiled at him as he looked at her, confused.

"Your heart was trapped in the darkness. The darkness brought me here. In order to free you, I filled your heart with as much light as I could," Sage said.

"You!" the king said. He seemed a bit taken aback.

"Yes, me. Your brother connived with the enchantress and together, they filled your land with darkness. Without you to put a stop to the growing rage and pain that he felt, without you to help keep his darkness balanced, he went crazy with power. Woe befalls anyone who should come here. They're immediately carried away by darkness, filled with hate, anger, envy, and frustration. The stench of it is so strong it has traveled to other worlds too."

The king frowned. He looked around the throne room. Bits of darkness still clung to the walls. He closed his eyes and levitated. Without a word, light began to fill the throne room, light so bright that Sage had to keep her eyes closed. The light exploded again, bursting forth from within the king. It traveled in every corner.

The king slowly descended until he was standing right in front of Sage. He offered her a brilliant smile.

"You came here with your friends last night. Did you not?" he asked.

"I did."

"How did you find us?" the king said.

"My bracelet led me here. It takes me to places like this," Sage said, waving her hand around the room. "Places that need a good cleaning from darkness."

The king chuckled. "My brother wasn't exactly evil. He just had a lot to deal with, you know. We're two halves of a coin. I give balance to my brother and my brother gives balance to me. Where I falter, he leads me. And where he falters, I lead him. Do you understand, Sage?"

"I do. My grandmother told me about balance. Like yin and yang. You're the yin to your brother's yang and your brother is the yang to your yin. He must know you're back."

"He knows. He felt it the moment I began to exist again. We're interconnected, you see. They will be here very soon," he said, leading Sage to the door.

Sage could see a man, a spitting image of the king, leading Harley and Juniper to the castle.

"Blake, my brother!" The king pushed open the doors and rushed outside. His brother ran towards him and engulfed him in a tight hug.

Where Drake had a white and gold armor, Blake had a black and gold armor. They were indeed two different sides of a coin, but unique. One without the other would cause imbalance, chaos. The energy radiating from them was balanced now; it was at peace.

Juniper and Harley caught up to them. They were not surprised to find her in the middle of the chaos. They both pulled her into a hug. When they broke apart, Juniper handed Sage her sneakers.

"You left them back in the room. How did you leave without any of us knowing?" Harley asked.

"Blake's darkness paid us a visit while we all slept at night. I believe he must have tried possessing you first, Harley. But you have a shield, it protects you, so it could not possess you. Then it went for Juniper next, but you have the gift to heal. You could heal any pain at all. So it stayed away from you. I, on the other hand, I look soft on the outside, but nobody knows what might happen on the inside."

"Oh, whoa. He possessed you and dragged you out of the room?"

"He took control of my body. While away, I met Eli. He sent me back here. The darkness brought me to the castle, and I found the heart and broke it free of its prison."

"And as such, I must thank you. Ask for whatever it is you want. If it is in our power, we shall grant it. We're forever grateful to you, child," Blake said.

He was different now. He seemed to glow. His eyes twinkled with joy as he held on to his brother. Sage felt satisfied, even though not completely. Something was still out of place.

"We need to return home, but we need to know why we cannot seem to find our way back home. There must be something here, keeping us back," Juniper said.

"You made mention of an enchantress. I have a feeling that she might be the reason why we are unable to get home. If you know anything about her, you must please share your knowledge with us," Sage stated.

"It is our only hope of getting home now," Harley added.

"Come with us. We will share our story with you," the king and his brother said.

Chapter Eleven

>) ● ((

"The enchantress is a part of us, just as much as we're a part of her. Long before now, we lived as inhabitants of Asgard. Born of the same womb, we grew together. Our mother called us the balance our Universe needed," King Drake said.

"We were born a few years apart. Unlike Drake and I, the enchantress had darkness in her as much as she had the light. She had superhuman stamina, almost like an Asgardian goddess. So, she wasn't any ordinary human, and she tried her best to stay away from anger," Blake added.

They were now in a grand hall in King Drake's castle. The walls were painted white, and golden curtains billowed in the quiet wind. Outside it was bright and not anywhere close to looking as dark as it had the previous day.

"Our sister was once of pure blood; she was a good witch. A healer. She would go on long pilgrimages, healing every sick person in her path. But she was weak too. Her hair was long and white, she had soft brown eyes, and blush-pink lips. Her voice could draw anyone in, man or beast. But just like everyone, she had a weakness of her own. She had a weakness that she battled with. She had an evil side that often times took control of her," Drake said.

"It was during one of her pilgrimages that she committed a crime against nature," Blake said.

"She killed someone, didn't she?" Sage asked.

"Yes. Our sister eventually became a high priestess. Many loved her. But for a person who battled evil, she also thrived on vengeance. Our sister was to be married to a fair young Asgardian warrior she had come to love. But he was murdered in cold blood by another."

Drake closed his eyes tightly, as if there were memories he wished to run away from.

"She swore vengeance. And vengeance empowered her. Drunk with pain and anger, she went off in search of the man who took her betrothed's life. She found him in a tavern. She ripped his heart out and watched it stop beating. And then she disappeared, never to be seen again."

"Except she wasn't truly gone, was she? She left to find a home for herself. A home where she would be most powerful. And you left to find her, but you ended up here, on this isle, and here you stayed for a long time!" Juniper stated.

"Our powers were immediately fused with this isle, yes. We made it into a home for ourselves, built it into something this beautiful. When the witch came, we realized it was our sister. But she was no longer pure. That one mistake that had been made years ago had completely destroyed her. She had become a seductress now. People began to whisper about her. They talked about how once she had been the high priestess loved by all and now, she was feared by everyone who came across her. Her eyes turned obsidian and her hair slowly turned black the same way her soul did," King Drake said.

Sage could hear the pain in his voice. They had tried their best to be good brothers. They had tried to protect their sister, but she was too overcome with hate, vengeance, and destruction. Now that she thought of it, love did not thrive very much in the other dimensions she had been in because the enchantress was slowly taking it away. She was trying to take it all away.

"Now that she's so powerful, she has changed her appearance. She now seduces both men and women. It doesn't matter to her. She commands animals too. They do her bidding. When she came here, she brought a black jaguar with glowing yellow eyes as well. It had the ability to walk through walls and leap over buildings. It could take the form of any other animal if she so desired," Blake said.

"Is there a way to identify her? How would we know who she is?" Sage asked.

"No matter what she looks like, the clothes she wears must remain an emerald green and it must be silk. Anything else will burn her. She has glowing black eyes and long dark wavy hair. There's a stone pendant chain headband around her forehead. In that stone lies all the evil powers she has acquired and uses. It is a crystal, a shimmering blood red ruby."

King Drake sat on his throne. He took off his crown and relaxed a bit. Sage could see his green eyes now. They were the same as Blake's. For someone who had just been brought back, Drake was a bit weak.

"The enchantress' powers are to conjure the elements. Do you understand me? She uses wind, fire, water, and air to get what she wants. She can also control your minds. It's going to be hard to try to destroy her. She still takes chunks of light from here. She's still turning it into darkness. But worse, she is still committing crimes against nature!"

119

The enchantress was the one nobody was brave enough to talk about in the other worlds. She was traveling through the worlds and taking what she wanted from them. In the Isle of Dragons, she had taken a bunch of their dragons. It was why the only dragon that they had seen was Chief Atkin's dragon. In the Isle of Man, she had captured all the princesses. In the Isle of Crystals, she was stealing their crystals from the crystal city, it was why the women left the city. In the Isle of Light, she took their light, her own brother, and kept him captive for ages.

"It's just like in old fairy tales. The evil enchantress uses her dark magic to cast spells and take whatever she needs, like capturing princesses and locking them away. Could you please tell us how she got all the power she possesses now? It can't just be from vengeance!" Harley said.

"No, it isn't. My sister has been summoning ancient powers in all the isles. She had been collecting them for herself. Remember that I was held captive here? My weakness was my love for my brother, and she used that against me. There's a vase hidden away from ordinary eyes. In it is all the captive princesses and the ancient powers from their kingdoms," Blake replied.

Drake looked at him. "How do you know about that?"

"She called me to her once, and I went. We were to make a deal; she would bring you back to me. But she instead fed me hatred and anger and sent me back here. It was how I began to feed others with darkness. The Universe gave me double of the pain I caused anyone. It was a thorn in my side. No matter how much I tried, I kept feeding and feeding the darkness until it completely consumed me."

"Oh, Brother. You must have gone through a lot!" Drake said.

"So, is there any way to stop your sister for good?" Sage asked. "It's the only way we can go back home, by stopping your sister. If you know a way that we can stop her, you must tell us now."

"There are many ways. If you're able to break the vase and free the princesses, you will be able to weaken her powers. The red ruby on her head, if you can destroy it first, you can stop her for good. But there's only one thing that can completely change her," Drake said.

"What's that?" Juniper asked him.

"If you can get her to shed a single tear. Ever since the darkness in her overwhelmed her completely, our sister never shed a tear. If you were to tap into her memories, it'll trigger her to shed a single tear. It'll break the darkness from within her and she will be completely free."

"How do we get to your sister?" Sage asked.

"You're sure you want to venture into this dangerous quest?" Blake asked.

"We haven't come all this way for nothing. We have lives back home that we need to get back to. We've been here for so long already! I miss home. And if defeating the enchantress is the only way back home, then we'll do it or die trying," Harley said.

The others agreed with him. King Drake turned to his brother. There was no convincing Sage and her friends to give up on the matter. They had journeyed so far after all.

"My sister lives on the other side of the isle. She claimed that part for herself. Only the bravest and strongest can pass through the thick darkness that covers her land. It is easier to get there than to leave. Are you sure you want to do this?"

"Yes," they all replied.

"May your quest be successful," Drake said.

He got up from his throne and walked toward Sage. He opened her palm and silently placed a dagger in her palm.

"This is made of light, pure light. It will shine in the darkest of places. Take it with you. It will lead you through her forest."

The dagger was indeed light. Sage held it out in front of the enchantress' forest. The darkness seemed to recoil at the sight of the light from the dagger. Sage led them through the forest.

"The trees have no leaves," Juniper whispered.

"No flowers, no sun, nothing. How could she have gone from being a healer to destroying nature this much?" Harley asked.

"I wouldn't know," Sage answered. "Her hands are tainted. She used magic to kill a man and spill blood. She committed a crime against nature."

"I honestly don't understand this whole crime against the earth thing," Harley said.

"The enchantress was a white witch, a healer. To heal another, your hands must be pure and untainted. You must not take the life of another. You must not even so much as lay a curse or hex on another, or it will consume you completely. It will take your good gifts and completely ruin them. You'll be left with nothing but pain," Sage replied.

A shiver ran through Harley's back as they got closer to the enchantress' castle. The castle was long and dark. It looked like something straight out of a villain movie scene.

"The negative energy here is the strongest I've ever felt since we started this journey. No wonder the trees have died, and the flowers are no longer existent," Sage said.

There were no front gates or anything, just a chain link bridge that took them a few minutes to cross.

"She must think no one would dare to pass through for her to leave this place unguarded," Harley said.

Sage chuckled. "Step one, never underestimate the enemy that you do not know."

A low, barely discernable laughter reverberated through the empty courtyard that they currently stood in.

"Your darkness doesn't scare me, you evil witch! Today your end begins! I will end you myself," came a loud voice.

Sage, Juniper, and Harley hid in a corner as a prince came into view. He looked handsome. He wore an armor that would at least protect his skin, but he had nothing to protect his mind. The enchantress would play with him for some time before deciding on what to use him for.

"He's skewered meat right now," Harley stated.

"We'll have to help him. But as far as we know, we don't have any grand plans on how to defeat her, so what are we going to do about Prince Charming over there?" Juniper asked.

Sage shrugged. She wasn't sure either. They had to do something, and really fast. Or the prince would indeed be gone faster than they could think.

"I like that you're brave! How were you able to get through the forest? Many have died trying while others gave up. There is something about you. I'm not able to place a finger on it," came the enchantress' sultry voice.

It was sugary sweet, the type that gave kids cavities. Sage shuddered. She didn't like this woman at all. It would be hard to hide that fact.

"I was able to pass through your forest because I had light with me! Now give me what I have come for?" the prince yelled.

"Oh." The enchantress cackled. "What is it that you're here for?" she asked him.

"She's nasty," Juniper whispered.

"I agree," Sage and Harley replied immediately.

"My fiancé. You have her captive. I need her back now. Not just her, but every other princess that you have stolen from the many kingdoms. You must free them all!"

A sudden dark cloud gathered out of nowhere in the middle of the yard. Out of it, came a woman. She looked young and beautiful. But the dark aura around her was too much. She walked toward the prince, but he swung his sword at her. It tore her skin, and she shrieked in pain. The prince didn't celebrate the cut and Sage saw why. The gash he had given her was slowly healing.

The prince fell back. "What is that?"

The enchantress began to hum a spell. The humming sound irritated Sage as the enchantress got closer to the prince. When the enchantress began to chant the spell out loud, Harley and Juniper blocked their ears.

It was obvious what the enchantress wanted to do. She wanted to keep the prince for herself. She wanted to corrupt him with her darkness and Sage knew they couldn't let that happen.

She started reciting the spell that would completely mesmerize him. She looked very determined. And Sage saw her determination as a weakness. The enchantress was lonely, and the loneliness was beginning to consume her as well.

"Bring together my prince and I, I summon him to be by my side, I am destined forever to be his bride, for together, we shall be divine!"

Darkness flowed out of her, eager to do her deed. As it got closer to the prince, Sage broke into a run.

She ran as fast as she could, and as she got closer, so did the dark cloud. At the last minute, Sage pushed him out of the way. They both fell to the ground.

"Oof!" Sage groaned as she hit the ground.

The enchantress broke out of her spell casting trance. She turned to Sage, anger flowing through her.

"You!" she yelled.

A sudden force grabbed Sage by her neck and lifted her off the ground. Sage struggled to breathe. She kicked harder and harder, but the enchantress did not relent.

"How dare you? What makes you think you can disrupt me and get away with it? How did you get to my castle?!" the enchantress asked, her voice filled with rage.

The prince got up and hid away from them. Just as Sage was on the verge of passing out, Juniper grabbed the wrist of the enchantress. Immediately, her healing energy began to flow through her into the enchantress.

It weakened her long enough for her to drop Sage back on the ground. Juniper let go when she began to feel the darkness from the enchantress. She ran to Sage's side and placed her hand on her.

"She almost killed you, Sage. We need to make her weak!" Harley yelled.

"Make me weak? You think you can make me weak?" the enchantress asked, clearly amused.

"In a castle lives an enchantress. In a vase lies her enchantments. Search her castle, destroy every vase. Leave none behind, so she might mend her evil ways."

At first nothing happened, so the enchantress began to cackle again. Her voice echoed throughout the castle and the forest. But she heard it just as much as they did when something shattered into pieces.

"No!" she yelled. "No! What have you done?!"

In one swift movement, Sage, Juniper, and Harley were caught up in midair. They had no control of their bodies anymore. Sage tried to move, but nothing would budge. Maybe this was it. Maybe this was where it would all end. Maybe it wasn't their place to stop the enchantress.

"But it is. It is your place to stop her. Only you can, Sage," a quiet voice said.

Sage opened her eyes. An Ascension Angel-like being was standing in front of her. Their voice was calming. A relief to the pain that Sage's physical body felt.

"How are you sure?" Sage asked him. They were standing in the middle of the meadow now.

"You could not possibly have come this far only to give up, Sage. Within you lies the purest of energy. Pure and untainted. You're divine, Sage. And only a divine being can stop the enchantress. Don't think, just focus. You're free of all bindings. Focus."

When Sage opened her eyes again, her hands began to glow with a bright light. The stronger the light grew, the stronger Sage felt. She turned her attention to focus on the enchantress. The red ruby on her crown needed to be destroyed. Sage pointed at the stone and the light from her hand hit it. A huge flash of light overpowered the courtyard. Sage's eyes glowed a brilliant white. From inside the castle, the vase in which she had trapped the princesses and their ancient powers levitated towards her.

Sage turned to the prince. "Break it!" she yelled.

He hurried out of hiding and smashed the vase with his sword.

"No!" the enchantress screamed.

Pieces of the broken vase went in every direction. The light from Sage lifted the goddess until she was above the ground. Then with one final force of light, the red ruby burst into tiny fragments, completely destroyed.

The enchantress dropped to the ground and so did Sage. Harley and Juniper ran toward her. The pieces of the broken vase began to bend before their eyes, turning into the lost princesses. Sage, Juniper, and Harley had never seen anything like it before.

They turned when they heard the high priestess begin to rise. Her eyes started to soften, and her black hair began turning white again. Her emerald-green dress turned a brilliant blue. But nothing prepared Sage for when the high priestess started to weep.

The light began slowly, starting from the high priestess before enveloping everything else. When Sage looked again, the princesses were gone, and the world had been restored to its natural order. Grasses grew underneath them, the trees came alive, and flowers began to bloom. There was every color of the rainbow. It felt so bright as they had been in darkness for so long. The colors shone like those of the crystal cave. Colors that human eyes had never seen before.

Chapter Twelve

)) ● ((

"I didn't think this place was this beautiful. Look at all the flowers!" Sage said.

Harley chuckled. "We just defeated a powerful enchantress and you're bothered about the flowers?"

"The flowers are important, you know. I've always loved flowers. So you can understand my excitement," she replied.

"I do," Harley said, brushing a lock of hair out of her face. They locked eyes again and Sage was afraid that if she looked away, he would disappear completely.

They were in one of the rooms in the castle. Sage got out of the incredibly soft bed. She wondered how long she had been asleep. She pulled on her sneakers before turning back to Harley.

"How long was I out?" she asked.

Harley got up from the bed and dipped his hands in his pockets.

"A couple of hours. I'm not sure. I really don't understand how time works here, you know."

"I do. Come on, let's go find Juniper. It's time for us to find our way home," Sage said, stretching her hand so Harley would hold it.

He smiled as he took her hand and they both left the room. Together, they walked down the castle halls. They ended up in the throne room, where the high priestess was making a crown of flowers for Juniper.

"Ah, you're here now, Sage. I hope you had a good rest?" the high priestess said the moment she saw them.

"I am well rested. I want to say thank you for your hospitality," Sage replied.

She caught Juniper hiding a smile after seeing Harley and her holding hands. Sage glowered at her, but the high priestess caught her attention.

"No. I must thank you. If you hadn't saved me from my own destruction, I would not be present here. I was blinded by so much pain that I forgot who I really was. The guilt and pain were thorns in my side, thorns buried very deep—thorns I could never reach to pluck out myself, but you did. This, I promise: I shall grant whatever it is that you ask of me."

"We ask nothing but that you show us the way home. We have succeeded in our quest. We ask to go back to the place we left behind," Sage said.

The high priestess frowned. "You do not wish to stay here? Is it not good enough?"

"It is not that, high priestess. Home is where the heart belongs. Home is everything. And we're not home. Home is where our loved ones reside. This cannot be our home," Juniper answered.

She dropped her crown of flowers and joined Sage and Harley where they stood. The high priestess nodded sadly. She understood what they wanted.

"Come with me," she said, leading them out of the throne room.

All three of them ran after her. As usual, Harley was faster. The high priestess led them through the forest. They could finally see how beautiful it looked with all its leaves and the birds. She led them to a field of flowers.

"You know what to do, Sage. It is time now," the high priestess said.

Sage nodded. She drew the circle once more, wide enough to fit three people. She closed her eyes and took a deep breath. This time, they didn't need to hold each other's hands. They were stronger now. They focused on calming their minds and using the power from within them to create a portal. Together, they began to chant the spell.

"From ancient times long past. Help me leave this vast land. Take me to a place where the flowers grow. Take me to where my ancestors sow. The seeds of new, a sky so blue, take me now through the heavens to you."

They continued to chant the spell until they felt the portal door open. The portal had a swirling, foggy, misty, and grayish color. They weren't sure where it would lead them. They weren't sure if it was the right portal to take them home or maybe it was the wrong one and it would take them somewhere even darker.

Suddenly, a glowing pure white light came in front of the portal. Sage had a feeling that it was Eli. With a beautifully calming voice, the entity called out to them.

"It's okay now. You are safe. It's time to return home. Your quest was successful."

They looked at each other. Juniper was the first to run towards the swirling white light. Then Harley grabbed Sage, and running toward the light, they jumped in together, hearts pounding, heads spinning. Sage turned to Harley. He was smiling. He must have noticed her looking at him as they jumped through the portal.

Their eyes connected. Sage had a feeling that she had never felt before. Her heart swelled as she looked at him. Her heart was expanding with a rush of loving energy. It was like the best feeling ever. She wasn't sure how to handle all the rush of emotions she felt in that moment. She looked at Harley again. This time, Sage saw something in his eyes that she had never noticed before. His soul seemed to be embracing her. It was a magical feeling. Intense. It felt like she couldn't breathe and move. Like time had stopped just for them. He had a loving, kind smile. Harley leaned over and kissed her on the lips. It was slow and sweet, with just the right amount of emotions pulsing through them. They held each other in a tight embrace for what seemed like hours.

Suddenly there was a bright light. Brighter than the light that had called them in. So bright they could hardly see. The portal vanished, and they found themselves on a bed of wildflowers that spanned miles and miles. In the middle of the field, a younger Sage played hide and seek with her mother. Her laughter echoed throughout the field and so did her mother's laughter.

Sage felt at peace now. Harley plucked a flower and gave it to her. They all laid back on the flowers. The sun seemed to be so bright in between the soft clouds and the bluest of skies they had ever seen. They were home. Finally.

Lunaa licked her face, her wet tongue wiping Sage's face effortlessly. Sage groaned and tried to move her cat aside, but the four-legged creature would not budge.

"You little! Leave me alone. I need to sleep!"

Lunaa got on her head and sat there comfortably. Sage pushed her off and sat up so fast her head spun. She looked at her grandfather clock. It was 11:11 AM.

Sage wiped her face and groaned. She stretched for a couple of seconds and then stood up. She staggered to her room and then her bathroom. The urge to pee was so strong. She shimmied out of her jeans, but they wouldn't move past her feet. She looked down to find out she was still in her sneakers.

"I went to bed with them on? Crap! Imagine what Juniper would say if she saw this," Sage mumbled.

She pulled off her shoes and then dragged her jeans off her feet. After she was done with answering nature's call, she got into the shower. The hot water touching her skin made her moan happily. The events of the previous night started to come back real fast. Sage stopped the water, a bit confused at her own memories.

Wasn't she locked in the storeroom with Juniper and Harley the previous night? So how did she get home? There was no way she could be dreaming! And what was this about traveling through different realms and saving them?

Nope. She needed to call Juniper. She got out of the shower and wiped herself dry. She felt a sudden craving for pizza. The craving was so strong that she threw on a regular band shirt and jean shorts and then grabbed her phone.

She rushed out of the house. The drive to John's pizza was a bit long. Sage took the time to think about everything she recalled. The memories were real; the emotions were real too. She felt at ease. She didn't despise her mother anymore, and she had kissed Harley!

Harley! How was that possible? Did Harley even like her? The Uber driver parked the car in the parking lot at Jim's pizza and then she got out of the car. She rushed through the doors, only for her eyes to catch Harley's.

The moment she saw him, a rush of emotions filled her up. She suddenly felt at home. She had never felt that way around him before. This was new and different, and it made her giddy. She didn't know when her legs carried her to his booth.

"Hi, Harley," she said, almost out of breath.

"Hello, Sage. You're here," he replied. "Oh, please have a seat."

Sage sat down. The aroma of pizza filled her nostrils, clouding her mind with images of her taking bites of the cheesy goodness.

Sage's phone buzzed in her pocket, and she picked it up. It was a text from Juniper.

"Meet me up at Jim's pizza? I'm on my way there. We need to talk! It's urgent."

Sage sent her a reply. "I'm there right now, with Harley. I met him here. I just had this crazy craving for pizza, and I got an uber out here."

"Are you texting Juniper?" Harley asked randomly. He sounded like he and Juniper were old buddies.

"Yeah. She says she's on her way here. I don't know what's going on, but this feels weird," Sage said.

"I thought I was the only one who felt that way. It feels like I just went on an incredibly long journey, and I need to eat enough for four people," Harley said.

"I feel the same way," Sage replied.

Harley stared at her. He smiled and stretched his hand across the table to hold her hand.

"Are you busy tomorrow? Would you like to go see a movie with me? Just me though, not the whole team."

Sage looked at Harley, blushing when she saw how honest he looked.

"Yeah, sure. I'd love to go see a movie with you. I'm never really busy on Sundays. I just hang out with Juniper," Sage replied.

"Okay, great. Seven sounds good to you?"

"Seven sounds perfect."

Sage gave his hand a tight squeeze. Just then, the door opened, and a hyper looking Juniper walked inside. Sage waved to get her attention. Juniper rushed to the table.

"I have reason to believe we all had the same dream last night," Juniper said as she sat in the booth quickly.

"Why? And how would that be possible?" Sage asked.

"Think about it. We were locked up in the storeroom last night. Do you remember who got us out? Or how we managed to get ourselves out? You don't, right?"

"Oh, that makes a lot of sense now that I think of it. I don't remember how I got on my couch or why I still had my sneakers on," Sage said.

"I don't either," Harley said.

"See? I suddenly woke up in my bed. I don't know how I ended up there. But it feels like I've been on a really long journey, and I only just returned. I'm telling you, we experienced something extraordinary today," Juniper said.

Someone served them a large pizza that Harley must have ordered before they got there. They each took a slice.

"So everything wasn't just some ordinary dream we were having?" Sage asked.

"Nope. I woke up this morning with a ring on my left pinky finger. I didn't remember putting it there," Harley stated, raising his hands to prove his point.

The ring shimmered in the light. Sage brushed it with the tips of her fingers. It pulsed with so much magic.

"I also have something of my own, a tattoo of a dove on my wrist," Juniper said.

She placed her hand on the table and truly, there was a tattoo of a dove on her wrist. It glowed when Sage brushed it.

"You now have the ability to heal, I can feel it. It's a strong energy, Juni. I've never felt it this strong before," Sage said.

"Last night, we had an adventure of a lifetime. We traveled through portals to different realms. We fought darkness and won.

We defeated an enchantress. We were given gifts. We discovered the most beautiful crystal cave. We met new friends along the way. It wasn't any dream. It actually happened. And I think this might not be the last time we go on an adventure like this. I for one, wouldn't mind going again."

Sage looked at Juniper. She had a small smile on her face. Sage knew she was far away. She was going to say something when the door opened again. Sage felt their presence before Juniper did. A kindred spirit.

"I think Ash is here, Juni. I think it's time you ask them out on a date. Harley already asked me out."

Harley stopped stuffing his face with pizza and smiled at Juniper. Juniper gasped.

"Tell me you aren't lying," she whispered.

"I'm not. We have a movie date tomorrow. Ask Ash and then we can make it a double date. Think about it."

Sage chuckled when Juniper got out of the booth. She and Harley watched her act clumsily for the first few seconds. Ash found her funny. They laughed at the silly jokes Sage was sure Juniper was already telling them.

"Do you think they'll say yes?" Harley asked her before gulping down a kombucha.

"I think they will. And I think they'll come on the double date with us. I'm certain Juni can sweep them off their feet."

Half an hour later, Juniper was back at their booth.

"What time are we meeting up tomorrow?" she asked.

"Seven. We are going to get dinner before the movie," Harley answered.

"Okay. Cool. I'll call you and get any information that I might need from you," Juniper said.

"I don't think you have my number," Harley said.

"I'll give it to her. No need to worry," Sage said.

"That's settled then."

It got dark pretty quickly. Sage didn't feel like doing a ritual. She sat outside on the porch swing and stared at the full moon for hours with Lunaa. She made up her mind to call her mother the next morning.

"I'm going to call Mum and tell her that I forgive her, Lunaa. I'll tell her that I know everything. That Grams already showed everything to me. And maybe, I'll convince her to go see Dad again. I want to see him. I want to know if he's still there."

Sage didn't know when sleep crept in, but she woke to her mother brushing her hair.

"Your grandmother paid me a visit, Sage. Do you know anything about that?" she asked, her soft melodious voice calming Sage.

"I don't know. She visits me as well. Every night she brushes my cheeks and says good night. She took me on a long adventure too," Sage replied.

"I'm sorry, Sage. I think it is time that you know why I did what I did years ago. It's time you know why I left you with your grandmother."

Sage turned to look at her mother. She had warmth in her eyes, and undying love too. Love so overwhelming that it engulfed Sage completely.

"I did not want to hurt you, Sage. Though I realize now that my actions have hurt you so much. They hurt me too. You see, Sage, your father and I could never be together. It broke me and for years, I tried to stay with you, to make you happy. Your happiness was more important. But then, I was beginning to break too. It got harder and harder to hide the cracks from you."

"But I would have stayed with you, nonetheless. Grandma told me you were running from something. I just wanted to hold you, to know you were there, but you weren't," Sage said. The sadness in her voice was evident.

"Everything that happened wasn't your fault, Sage. None of it was your fault. I was wrong for leaving you behind. I tried so hard to look for peace elsewhere, but it was near impossible. I loved your father and even today I still love him. But if I stayed, I would have hurt you," her mother said. She dropped the brush and pulled Sage into her arms.

"You won't leave again, will you?" Sage asked.

"I promise, I won't. I won't leave again. This time, I'll stay and try to fix every single thing that has been broken."

Sage felt soft lips press against her forehead. The smell of lavender and honey tea filled her senses. She closed her eyes and fell into a beautiful slumber.

When she opened her eyes again, she was still on the swing, Lunaa right beside her. It was daybreak already.

Sage heard a car drive down in front of her grandmother's cottage. She recognized its owner.

A figure with long flowing hair climbed out of the car holding a spell book with three crystals attached. The crystals were shaped like crescent moons. "Forget something?"

"Mum!"

ESTB 2021

Lilyleaf11

PUBLISHING CO

Whether in the ocean, a pebble, a gemstone, or yourself, the
energy of the universe permeates all.
— *Sarah Bartlett*

You don't have to wander around in silk robes burning sage with
crystals tied to your head to find the power within.
— *Jessica Marie Baumgartner*

Maybe one day,
after centuries,
we can become brilliant gems
in crystal caves
and we will be immortal after all
— *Keelie Breanna*

Moon Love
She held the moon
The way
She held her heart,

As if it was the only
Light that could guide
Her through the
Darkest nights.
—*Chrissie Pinney*

Moon Child
She was, in fact, a child of the moon.
Wondering around aimlessly, in the dark. Bringing light, to
everyone around her.
—*s & a*

You be the sun.
I'll be the moon-
Just let your light
Come shining through,
And when night comes.
Just like the moon.
I'll shine the light
Right back to you
—*Unknown*

You don't always need a plan. Sometimes you just need to breathe,
trust, let go and see what happens.
— *Mandy Hale*

About the Author

Layna B is a lively adventurous soul, who mixes real life with imagination to create fun, fantasy, and sci-fi novellas. She is part of the creative team at Lilyleaf11.com a little online boutique store in Red Beach, New Zealand. When she's not writing she loves doing yoga, meditation, gym workouts and hanging out at the beach. She's an avid crystal collector and has a huge range of colors and types. She loves helping people find true happiness. She has a vivid imagination and loves to create other worlds and characters that excite and delight.

Want more information about Lilyleaf? Visit lilyleaf11.com to join the mailing list and receive a free PDF on crystal properties and how to cleanse your crystals. Sign up for emails to get the latest news. You can unsubscribe anytime.

Follow us on:

Instagram @lilyleaf11
Facebook @lilyleaf11
Pinterest @lilyleaf11
Contact- hello@lilyleaf11.com
Website- Lilyleaf11.com
Layna Belle - laynab.com (Fiction)
Indi B- indibauthor.com (Non-Fiction)
Book- souluniversebook.com
Book/Journal ideas- myinneruniversebook.com

About Lilyleaf11 Publishing Co.

Lilyleaf11 Publishing Co. is a boutique company that was designed to allow Lilyleaf to independently publish books to help others on their own journey through life. We would love people to live their best life having fun along the way. We have non-fiction and fiction books available. Keep your eyes peeled for more books arriving soon.

If you need any more information, please contact:
hello@lilyeaf11.com

Check out Lilyleaf11.com

Follow us on social media
Instagram @lilyleaf11
Pinterest @lilyleaf11
Facebook @lilyleaf11

Sign up for emails on Lilyleaf11.com and receive a free crystal cleanse and properties pdf.

Check out more books by Layna Belle:
Laynab.com
These link to the Lilyleaf11.com website where you can see new books available

Check out non-fiction titles by Indi B:
Indibauthor.com